Thicker Than Water

Water

(Book 3 in *The Grayson Trilogy*)

GEORGIA ROSE

1st Edition Published by Three Shires Publishing

ISBN: 978-0-9933318-6-2 (paperback)

ISBN: 978-0-9933318-7-9 (ebook)

www.georgiarosebooks.com

Cover design by the team at SilverWood Books
(www.silverwoodbooks.co.uk)

British Library Cataloguing in Publication Data

A CIP catalogue record for this book is available from the British Library.

The Grayson Trilogy

A Single Step

Before The Dawn

Thicker Than Water

A Note from the Author

This is for you, you lovely person who has kindly chosen this book to read. Please note, if you haven't already, that this is the third book in a trilogy. I strongly advise you to read *A Single Step* and *Before The Dawn* before you begin this one. While *Thicker Than Water* is a complete story in itself I will not be rehashing a lot of back story from the first two books and you'll be missing many of the reasons why characters are where they are or behave as they do. If you think this is a blatant attempt by an author to sell more of their earlier books, well perhaps it is...*but* if you go to find the other books, the prices are not to your liking and you don't want to buy them, please contact me (details at the back of this book) and I will be delighted to get a copy to you. I only want you to get the best experience of reading *Thicker Than Water* that you can.

Now, a word of warning: I have included an additional section at the end of this novel. No, I haven't done that thing where the author puts the first chapter of their next book in at the end to tempt you into further purchases, but I have added a little something extra for you. A little something special, if you will. No skipping ahead now, no peeking, you need to approach this at the right speed and it is what I've wanted to do ever since I started writing this trilogy. I think it may well be my Marmite moment: you may love it, or the other thing. Who knows? I have been told it is risky, but what is life without a few risks along the way? I hope you enjoy.

Thank you,

Georgia

This book is dedicated to you, and all my other lovely readers.

I never thought I'd find you so thank you for taking the chance on me.

Then you will know the truth, and the truth will set you free.

John 8:32

Chapter 1

I was in denial.

Ignoring what was happening to me, I closed down, unable to acknowledge the truth of it. Knowing if I did, if I faced what was coming, if I opened that box, all the evils I'd spent so much time locking away deep inside would be loose once more. I feared what impact they might have on me now, and was afraid of what would become inevitable. It was a foolish way to behave, but that's what I did and I got on with my life.

It was early October. Trent and I had been married a month or so, and after the dramas of the summer – Zoe, 'the incident', the crazy time we'd had after as we'd rushed towards our wedding, all of that a blur to me now – our life was calm again and I liked that. I liked that a lot, and I didn't want anything to mess it up.

I use the term 'calm' loosely because it's always relative to what others might consider it to mean. To us it meant I was back at work, busy with keeping the horses fit and the yard running smoothly. That was calm. It also meant Trent had disappeared off for a week with Cavendish as, after the summer's excitements and distractions, they'd restarted their efforts to close down the illegal operations of the Polzins' organisation. For some people this might not seem that calm; for us it was how our life together was.

We'd had a couple of days as our honeymoon when we'd hidden away from the world in the tree house and spent most of that time in bed, never able to get enough of each other. But with the honeymoon over it was business as usual.

I watched Trent now as he crossed the yard towards me. Tall, dark and athletic, his hair wild and unruly, he pushed his sleeves up over strong forearms with hands that I wanted to feel on me. As he came closer I was treated to an irresistible smile that lit up his dark blue eyes. He leaned down to greet Susie and made a fuss of her as she, hussy that she was, rolled onto her back and bared her belly to him. I put the bucket of water I was carrying into the stable and turned to greet him. As we met his arms wrapped around me and held me close, moulding me to his body.

"Hello, wife," he mumbled into my neck. He'd taken to calling me this; I wasn't keen and was trying to break the habit, but it was difficult to chastise him when he was so enthusiastically happy with life at the moment. He had been ever since I'd said yes when he'd asked me to marry him. I'd made him happy, I knew that. Marriage had been important to Trent – less so to me, but it had made all the difference to him. He was content and settled and he did everything he could to make me feel the same way.

"Hi," I murmured back, loving his hug, the feel of his body hard up against mine and his lips as they travelled across my skin, making their way to and eventually finding my mouth. He'd got back the previous night, late, and surprised me. We were both now suffering from a lack of sleep.

He pulled back and peered at me, frowning as he did so. "You look a bit tired." Which is just what every woman wants to hear.

"Whose fault's that?" I responded firmly.

"Hmm…" I could feel him studying me closely. "There's nothing else?"

"Nothing else," I lied as I pushed him away from me, feigning a need to get on. He changed the subject, sensing my reluctance to share.

"So, do you have any plans for later?"

I'd picked up the emptied buckets from the last stable and went to refill them as I answered. "I've got to bring the horses in, get them finished off, then I was planning on heading to the gym. Why do you ask?"

"I need to finish off clearing my stuff out of the apartment for Carlton and Greene. They're itching to get in there so I thought I'd do that this evening. Do you want to come over after the gym and I'll cook?"

"Sounds good. I'll see you later." I leaned over to give him a kiss goodbye and returned to my bucket-filling as he left. I felt him look back at me; I knew he was checking on me, but I didn't return his gaze.

I wandered wearily out to the paddock to bring the horses in. There was the scent of autumn in the air: multi-hued leaves ablaze on the trees; the ploughed fields that surrounded the estate, earthy and rich; the woody smoke of a bonfire carried on the light breeze. Monty and Zodiac were already waiting for me so they came in first. After checking them over I put them in their stables for the night before returning for Regan and Benjy.

I went to get changed for the gym, then sat on the edge of the bed and wondered if I could be bothered to go for the workout. I felt drained, but told myself it was due to the lack of sleep the previous night. Forcing myself to stand, I went downstairs and checked Susie was settled in her basket before grabbing my keys and heading out the door.

It was already dark, but I walked to the Manor using that journey as my warm-up. After 'the incident' when men from the Polzin organisation had entered the estate, I'd been wary for a while, nervous of being out and about on my own, but gradually I'd settled down again. Security was tighter on the estate now, and intel via the security services was monitored for any indication that there was likely to be another attack. Trent had been right. Orlov, an enforcer for the organisation, and Anatoly, the youngest of the Polzin brothers, had retreated back to where they had come from, and so far there had been no further sight or sound of them. Long may that continue, I thought as I strode towards the Manor.

I walked up to the gym door and steeled myself before entering. I wasn't up for this, but went in anyway and waved cheery hellos to the few others already hard at work. Carlton and Greene were both there and I stopped to exchange a quick word with Greene, who was on the cross-trainer. She was supremely fit – everyone here worked out, but she took it to another level, rather like Carlton. I suspected they were in some sort of internal competition with each other, honing their bodies, each muscle toned and working to its maximum potential. Definite contenders for the gorgeous young couple awards, should there be such a thing. Greene had once told me she needed to be this fit in order to keep up with Carlton; I really didn't want to think about that, but the image was reinforced by Trent arranging to move out of his apartment for them. Apparently their bedroom antics were causing problems for the rest of their flatmates; they needed space of their own.

Greene was going for it now, striding out and making me tired just looking at her.

"How's it going?" I enquired.

"Fine, nearly done. You all right?" Her words, compact, shot out in time with her breaths.

"Yeah, okay."

She frowned, her head tilted to one side as she studied me, not breaking her stride. "You sure? You don't seem very…up." I could sense her concern. "You're not coming down with something?" I shook my head, then felt an arm up and around my shoulder as I was hugged into Carlton's sweaty body and assailed by the hard-working masculine scent that accompanied it, which wasn't entirely unpleasant.

4

"Hey, how are you doing?" He took one look at me and furrows creased his brow. "You look tired."

I glared at him.

"Don't tell her that, Carlton," Greene scolded. "Nobody wants to hear that." She was starting to slow down and looked at me more closely. Pulling a face, she then commented, "You do look a bit peaky, though. Sure you're okay to work out?"

That made my mind up for me.

"Actually, I don't think I am. Maybe I am coming down with something," I lied, again. "I'll give it a miss and go over to help Trent clear out his place for you instead. Bet you're looking forward to moving in?"

"Can't wait," Carlton replied enthusiastically. "We haven't had much privacy to date," and he grinned salaciously at Greene, who rolled her eyes back at him.

"I'll probably see you tomorrow then for the big move in." I smiled at them as we said our goodbyes then shrugged his arm from my shoulder as I turned to leave. Though relieved with my decision not to work out, I did feel a little guilty for copping out so easily.

I walked across the courtyard and let myself into Trent's apartment – at least for one more night – and called out to him. I could smell dinner cooking the moment I entered. Nausea tightened my throat and becoming slightly lightheaded I swallowed quickly trying to shake off the feeling as Trent came to greet me. Having visited the gym already he was freshly showered, his hair still wet.

"I wasn't expecting you yet, wi...er, Emma. What happened to the workout?"

I ignored his question, though appreciated the correction, and instead asked my own: "What're you cooking?"

"Lasagne, green salad, garlic bread. All your favourite things." And they were too, usually, but now my stomach turned over, a rush of heat flushing my face. It was the smell. I swallowed again, clearing my mouth, my throat, and crossed to sit down on one of the leather settees in the sitting room.

Trent watched me carefully. "What's the matter, Em? You don't look so good."

"I'm fine." I waved away his concern. "I thought I'd skip the gym, it's no big deal."

"Okaaay, that's not like you…" He let that hang.

"I feel a bit tired, that's all," I snapped, then hesitated. "Sorry, I didn't mean to bite your head off. I'll just lie here while you get dinner ready and have a rest. I'm sure I'll be fine."

Temporarily satisfied with this he disappeared into the kitchen. Music played softly and I lay back, concentrating on calming the contents of my stomach. I hadn't realised I'd fallen asleep until Trent was gently waking me up.

"Come on, sleepyhead, time for dinner." He encouraged me to my feet. Shaking myself awake, I followed him into the kitchen. Big mistake. One look at the table, all set and ready to go; one look at my plate; one look specifically at the green salad on my plate and my stomach lurched. Saliva flooded my mouth as the blood drained from my head.

"Excuse me," I mumbled and, clamping my hand across my mouth, I ran from the kitchen towards Trent's bedroom and headed for the bathroom. I skidded to my knees as I reached the toilet, my stomach heaving, my guts contracting as I puked. But despite retching violently, not much came up; I'd not eaten for hours.

Then, as quickly as it had come on, it was over. I sat back on my heels, wiping away the sweat that had broken out on my forehead, then leaned up against the wall, breathing deeply, my body calming as the shaking subsided. I drew my knees up to my chest, wrapping my arms around them as I hugged them to me, willing myself to hold it together. I rocked slowly, tears forming, knowing I should not be feeling like this.

"Can I come in, Em? Are you okay?" came from outside the bathroom. Trent didn't wait for an answer. The door opened wider, then, taking one look, he joined me on the floor, wrapping his arms around me. "Hey, hey, hey…what's the matter? Are you ill?"

A tear spilled over, wetting my cheek, and he wiped it away as I shook my head, closing my eyes, wanting to look anywhere but at him.

"Talk to me, Em, you're worrying me." I could hear the concern in his voice and I took a deep breath, blowing it out, hoping it would help me to control myself, and my tears. Then I turned to look at him, hesitating, wanting to put off the moment – wanting to avoid it forever, preferably – knowing that what I said next would change everything.

It was unavoidable.

"I'm pregnant." And I watched his face change, seeing what I knew I would see in it, what I knew I should see in it, never having had any doubt: joy. Pure unadulterated joy flitted through his eyes, lighting him up as if an internal switch had been flicked on.

"Emma, that's wonderful news. I mean, I know we hadn't been trying, we hadn't planned on this, but…" His voice petered out as he looked at me. I smiled back him, but couldn't stop my lip from trembling. My eyes I knew were shiny, brimming with the tears that were yet to fall. I hated myself in that moment, stealing this from him, and leaned forward to kiss his cheek to try to make it all right.

He continued, his voice quiet, "I'm so sorry, I wasn't thinking about how this would affect you…that was thoughtless of me."

"No, it wasn't." I shrugged it off, unable to say more. I knew, however hard he tried, he couldn't truly understand what I'd gone through when I'd lost Eva, and what this was doing to me now. I remembered finding out I was pregnant with Eva and how excited I'd been; how excited *we'd* been – Alex had been thrilled. But that joy had all been eclipsed by the anguish that followed when she died.

Trent had done a good job of making Eva part of our lives. He asked questions and we talked about her. This was different, though. This was going to be taking me right back to the beginning, reliving each moment of pregnancy that I'd experienced before but with nothing but raw painful memories to show for it. Emotional at the best of times, I was exhausted by the very thought of what I was going to have to face.

Now I'd spoken those words out loud however it was as if they'd been a magic spell that had awoken something deep inside. I could feel the memories shifting, uncoiling from within as if they were sleeping serpents writhing around each other, each waiting to rise up into my consciousness like sharpened sticks ready to cause me pain with each prod.

I heard him sigh, and his arms loosened as he slumped away from me. "Is part of it that you don't want *my* baby?" My heart sank. I should have known he'd make some comparison with Alex. A while ago now I'd told him that Alex 'was the man I once loved so much that I chose him to have a child with'. Clearly Trent had not forgotten.

"No, Trent, that's not it, that's not it at all. You will be a great father and you know how much I love you but we didn't choose this, we didn't decide, but it's happened and it's…" I was searching for an easy way to explain "…it's just that I'm not ready for it. I haven't prepared myself. I haven't had time. We've never even talked about having a child, and perhaps we should have done."

"You must have known I would want children, you see how I am with Sophia and Reuben. I know we hadn't discussed having a baby, but equally you've never told me you didn't want another child, so I suppose I'd assumed that one day we would have one. I just didn't want to discuss it yet, it was too soon."

And I nodded. That was my point: it was too soon. He was great with Cavendish and Grace's children, and I couldn't blame him for not bringing it up. We'd only been together a few months and I'd made sure I was on the pill – *I was on the pill* repeated slowly in my mind. And now that my mind was open and acknowledging my situation I questioned how this could have even happened. I took the pill religiously every morning. I woke, got up, and took it. Like clockwork, every morning. Of course – I groaned as I realised there had been a morning I hadn't taken it. A morning when, instead of waking comfortably in a nice warm bed, I'd been bringing in an aircraft to land at RAF Loreley instead, the climactic point of 'the incident'. I bore the scars to prove it: a slash across my upper arm from Orlov's knife; a fainter one on my neck. I had missed taking my pill once and that had been all that was needed.

"How long have you known?" Trent questioned.

"A little while," I admitted reluctantly and looked away from him, studying my hands. "I haven't allowed myself to believe it until now – until I couldn't ignore it any longer."

"Why not?" Trent was curious as to where my mind was and I couldn't blame him. It was all over the place, but there were two main areas of concern and I knew he wouldn't let up on me until I'd shared. I sighed, knowing I was going to have to spill.

"What if she thinks I'm replacing her?" Eva was still very much a part of my life; she occupied many of my thoughts. After shutting her away in my heart and keeping her to myself for so many years, I'd been encouraged by Trent to talk about her. I wasn't crazy; I knew she was dead, but I still felt close to her as if she were merely living in some parallel world. I knew I couldn't get to her right now, but she'd continue to live there eternally until the day came when we would be reunited. If you believe in such things you might call the place heaven. I didn't, but I still thought that's where she was. How could I think of her as being anywhere else?

She'd come to me, not only in my dreams, when I got to hold her in my arms, inhale her smell and feel her warmth, the softness of her hair and the smoothness of her skin, but during 'the incident'. When my life had been truly in danger I had seen her, as if in that extreme moment the walls between her world and mine had become thinner and she'd been able to reach me. I realised I'd been hallucinating, but it had felt so real. To me she was only just on the other side, and I couldn't help but feel she would know and this pregnancy would affect her.

Trent took a long pause before replying. "From everything you have told me about her, Em, I can't imagine her thinking that for one moment. She was strong and kind and she loved you. If she were still here I'm sure she would have enjoyed having a little brother or sister, and she would have shared you then. She will always have a place in your heart, Em, so don't think of it as you replacing her, but more of her sharing you with someone else."

"Yeah." I agreed. "That's a good way to think of it, a positive way..." I was silent and he probed further. He knew there was more.

"Don't you think she would want you to be happy?"

I pondered on this. It was a moot point as the baby was already on the way, but I had to face it: would having another baby make me happy? Ever since I lost Eva I hadn't believed I deserved to be happy and for a long time, not wanting to move on and thinking I had to keep the wounds open and raw to keep her fresh in my mind, I continued to seek out the pain. Trent had helped me to see beyond that and made me realise I could let it go and allow other things into my life. It didn't mean I thought any less of Eva but it had meant I'd come so far out of the depths of depression I'd now reached a point where I didn't want to go backwards. However, I could only see a future ahead that would be tormented with fear over the safety of the child. I could see myself becoming over protective, restrictive on what he, or she, did, rushing to the doctor with the slightest thing. How could that be a good environment in which to bring up a child?

I voiced these concerns to Trent, finishing with, "What if I can't do this?" My voice was tight and hoarse. "I failed before, Trent. What if I can't keep this child alive? I…" I choked, my voice petering out as the tears came. I'd said it out loud, my biggest fear, and Trent hugged me to him, rocking and soothing me and letting me cry it out.

"I know it's not going to be easy, Em," he murmured, "but we're in this together and we'll work it out as we go along." He pulled back, his fingers running along my jawline as he tipped my chin up so he could meet my eyes. "One step at a time, yeah?"

"Yeah," I agreed, feeling stronger with his reassurance. I often forgot how good it felt to be no longer alone.

Smoke curled lazily from the cigar propped up in the cheap glass ashtray. He sat in the chair, facing what was meant to be a dressing table – if anyone who required one had been present. As it was it substituted as a desk in the absence of anything more suitable in the small and depressingly worn-out hotel room he currently called home.

His right hand, encased, as it and its partner so often were, in a close-fitting vinyl glove, was wrapped around a tumbler holding bourbon, a bottle of which he'd brought with him. This wasn't the sort of establishment that would have the stock to provide him with what he wanted, and he didn't need to bring himself to the attention of anyone with requests that might be remembered.

The hotel was large and run down, nothing having been spent on its decoration in, he reckoned, the last twenty years. There was a high turnover of guests, some staying one night, passing through; some, he suspected, staying an hour, such were the clientele and the area in which the hotel was located. Money changed hands for blind eyes to be turned. This was a place where nobody cared for customer satisfaction, where guests were anonymous and forgotten, which suited his purposes. This was why he'd brought his own bottle. Reaching for it now, he refilled his glass.

Chapter 2

The following morning I felt fine and set about my normal routine. Trent disappeared up to the Manor to do whatever it was he did there while I exercised Regan and led Benjy out first. Although it was dry and sunny there was an autumn chill in the air and I'd wrapped up warmly. Susie joined us, scampering back and forth through the fallen leaves wherever the scents and trails led her. We kept half an eye on each other, the distance between us never becoming too great.

I rode Monty out next, leading Zodiac, and had a livelier time of it. Monty could often be flighty, but that morning he was spooked by the most ridiculous of things. Admittedly he had good cause to jump when a pheasant launched itself skyward right under his nose, but from then on he was skittish, quivering beneath me if leaves fell too close or anything moved in the undergrowth. He shied time and time again, suddenly suspicious of clumps of grass, trees, ditches, logs, plants – nature, in fact, in all its glory. I rode him back towards home on the road in the hope of calming him down as he was breaking out in a muck sweat. Zodiac, who was getting little enough attention as I had my hands full, was being dragged along by Monty's antics having no choice but to put up with it.

I managed to free a hand as we jogged sideways and raised it to wave at Cavendish as he drove slowly past to let him know I was all right. He replied to my grin with one of his own. As we arrived back at the stables, I'd barely dismounted when Trent's truck drove into the yard. It stopped, or rather it screeched to a halt, and he jumped out, slamming the door behind him as he strode towards me. *Uh-oh.*

"What the fuck do you think you are doing?" he demanded.

"My job," I countered, my defences up. He didn't swear often; it was an indicator of his anger when he did, and right now I knew he was really, really mad. Like the time he had caught me riding out without my back protector on – now that was a bad day. "What's the problem, Trent?"

"The problem is that Cavendish got back and told me he'd just seen Monty dancing sideways down the road with you."

"Oh, it's not a problem. That's the way he is sometimes."

This was nothing unusual for me so I was surprised when he came back with, "You obviously can't carry on working now. I should have thought of this earlier, stopped you from going out."

"Trent, you can't stop me, this is my job."

"Of course I can, I'm the estate manager."

Oh, don't do that, I thought. Don't pull that rank stuff with me.

I tried to reason. "There's no need for me to stop, Trent. I'm perfectly safe and you're being overprotective."

"Emma, you've fallen from a horse more than once since being here, and I'm not going to risk it." He was right, but I tried to retaliate, even though I realised I was on shaky ground with my argument.

"I'm not the one in the most dangerous occupation, Trent. You're going to be a parent as well, and I don't suppose you're about to give up your work."

"But I'm not the one carrying our child, Emma!" He took a deep breath before continuing. "If I were I would give it up in a heartbeat."

So now I felt bad. I knew he was right, only I couldn't let it go.

"I am not giving up my job, Trent, that's unfair. I need to work, I need to be around the horses."

He paused, releasing his held breath, and nodded; he knew how much they helped my state of mind. His eyes closed briefly as he calmed.

"Look, Emma, this baby has already come through a lot just to get this far, and it's our duty to do all we can to protect it."

"What do you mean?"

"You were on the pill..." he stated, "you missed it one day and you're pregnant. What do you think the chances are of that?" I shook my head; I didn't know. "Our baby has already survived you being kicked across the gym by Turner – had you thought of that?" I hadn't. He took hold of my shoulders and gave me the full effect of his penetrating gaze. "This baby, our baby, really wants to be born and we have to do our best to make sure that happens." I nodded. I knew that and I knew he was right, but...

"I have to work, Trent. The stuff that is building up in my head because of the whole baby business is going to drive me crazy otherwise...please." My voice sounded pleading, which I hated.

"Okay." And my hopes were raised for a moment. Was he going to relent? Not, it seemed, entirely. "I'll tell you what, how about a compromise?"

"You want to negotiate?" I smiled; we'd trodden this track before. "What have you got?"

He considered me, his head tilted.

"I don't want you to ride or handle the horses at all." I was horrified he was taking such a hard line, but knew I'd get nowhere with the riding issue. That was a non-starter and he had a good point. I had fallen off before, more than once since being here, and if that happened and I lost the baby I would never forgive myself. But I needed to do more than he was offering, which was next to nothing.

"So…what? That leaves me able to do a bit of gentle tack cleaning, does it? Oh, and the mucking out?"

"Actually I don't want you mucking out either. I'd forgotten about that. It's too strenuous for you." His face broke into a grin as I scowled at him. I knew – at least I hoped – he was winding me up. He must have known there was no way I would go for that. He knew I hated accepting help from anyone so I assumed he was starting from a low base and hoping for too much.

"That's no compromise at all. Here's what I will give you. I will stop riding…and that is it. Everything else I will continue doing. I will be careful, I will keep myself safe, but I will go mad if I do not work."

He frowned.

"And if you're ill? Or later on when you get too…big?" and he waved his hands in the general direction of my body.

"Then I'll worry about that when it happens and arrange cover as required. Please, Trent, let me carry on with everything else." I needed him to be on my side with this. He was right: he did have the authority to stop me, but I hoped for the sake of our relationship he was not about to.

"All right…I'll run it past Cavendish and talk to Carlton and Greene and see what we can come up with."

"Thank you," I said with relief, "although…"

"I know, this means we are going to have to tell people. At least those three and Grace. I know it's earlier than you wanted."

"I haven't even been to the doctor yet, Trent, had it confirmed."

"There's not any doubt, is there?"

"No, not really…" At that moment a wave of nausea rolled through my stomach as if in confirmation.

"We'll go to the doctor tomorrow, it's your day off anyway. We'll tell the others this afternoon."

"Only those four?"

"Only those four," he confirmed. "Do you want some help now? Or are you okay? You look a bit pale again."

"I'm fine, Trent. I'll see you at the apartment this afternoon."

He gave me a quick hug and pulled away.

"Okay, see you later." Then as he walked away he called back over his shoulder, "Oh, and don't think you'll be carrying anything this afternoon."

I sighed. If he was set to continue in this overprotective mode this was going to be the longest pregnancy ever. I turned back to Monty whose reins I'd been holding throughout this exchange and proceeded to untack him. I didn't like the thought of not being able to ride again for so long but told myself it was only for a few months and it wasn't as if I had much choice.

I couldn't eat anything other than some dry crackers for lunch and even they churned uncomfortably in my stomach as I drove to the Manor. I parked and walked up the few steps to Trent's old apartment door, which stood open. It looked as though the moving, such as it was, had already taken place: the sitting room was stacked with boxes, many hands having made light work of it. The furniture was staying anyway, so it had only been Carlton and Greene's personal items that had to be brought over .

I could hear voices from the kitchen, and as I entered Cavendish was popping the cork from a bottle of champagne. As froth spilled into glasses I greeted everyone, and once the drinks had been handed out, Cavendish toasted the couple in their new home. Despite the toast I knew a drop would never pass my lips. The moment I smelt it my stomach heaved, and then of course there was Trent, who I knew would be watching.

Trent waited until the celebration had passed then cleared his throat. If I wasn't already feeling nauseous, I would have definitely been feeling sick right about now, purely with the anticipation.

"Erm, I'm sorry if this is stealing your moment," he indicated with his glass to Carlton and Greene, "but Em and I have got something to tell you and it needs to be today. Sorry." All eyes turned to him.

"No problem, Trent, what's going on?" Carlton had been the one to voice everyone's curiosity.

"For reasons that I hope you all understand, we need you to keep this to yourselves for the time being. We're adjusting to the news ourselves…and obviously Emma's…well Emma's…"

"Oh, for God's sake, man, spit it out," Carlton exclaimed, and Trent glared at him before continuing.

"We're having a baby." Then he elaborated, in case any of them didn't get it. "Emma's expecting a baby."

There was a moment of silence, for the words to be processed by our friends. A slightly awkward hesitation where they tried to assess how I was reacting and coping with this news. It was only a split-second hesitation, but it was there. There were no loud exclamations of joy, but I could feel their excitement.

"Oh, Emma," and Grace hugged me to her fiercely. "Are you okay?" I saw Cavendish shaking Trent's hand and congratulating him, which made me feel happier.

"I'm fine. Nauseous, but fine," I told her and smiled as she pulled away and held me at arm's length to inspect me. Hugs followed from all the others and they raised their glasses in another toast. This time I made no pretence; I couldn't even bear to hold the glass.

Once everyone had settled down again, Trent cleared his throat before getting to the point. "So the problem is…well, why we needed to speak to you is because of the horses. I don't want Emma to be riding anymore…"

"Ahh," interrupted Cavendish, "now I understand. That's why you flew out of the office this morning, because of how I'd just seen Monty behaving with her. Quite right, Trent. We can't have her riding anymore."

"I still want to do everything else with the horses as long as I'm fit and well," I jumped in, clarifying, wanting to make sure of my position.

A discussion followed. It was agreed that for the time being Carlton and Greene would exercise the horses each day, and Cavendish and Grace would take them out whenever they could, and we'd go from there. I was pleased it had been sorted out so simply.

We left the couple to get settled in their new home and walked out with Cavendish and Grace.

"We're delighted for you both," said Cavendish as we parted. "Let us know if we can do anything."

Although I'd known them for a while now, I'd grown closer to both Cavendish and Grace since our wedding, which I supposed was only natural as they were such good friends of Trent's. Despite their titles and wealth, they were very hands on with the estate work and it hadn't taken me long to realise that, while Cavendish had inherited the estate, it was Grace who was its heart. We usually had supper with them, or they with us, at least once a week.

It had been at the first of these suppers following our honeymoon that I'd tackled Cavendish about who the guardian angel watching over Grace and the children could be.

At our wedding I'd overheard Cavendish feeding back the highlights of the ballistics report from the night of 'the incident' to the boys. As Grace, the children and I had been leaving the yard on the horses our escape route had been blocked by a man with a gun. This man had been killed, right in front of us, with one shot to the head. The main point of interest for me had been in the anomaly – whoever had shot the gunman appeared to have played no further part in the action that evening. He wasn't one of our people, and, as he'd shot one of them, it didn't seem as if he was one of the enemy either.

Of course I'm saying he – it could just as well have been a she.

Trent, Cavendish and Grace had all been surprised when I'd raised the question at supper. Grace hadn't known anything of the report so had to be filled in, and although Trent had filled me in on some of the detail he'd had no idea quite how much I'd overheard.

Cavendish had listened patiently to me and then fixed me with the piercing blue of his eyes for a long moment as if I were an object of some curiosity. The crease between his eyes furrowed deeper as he frowned. He'd told me they had no idea who had taken that shot, and then he'd asked me something rather strange.

"What makes you think it was Grace and the children the guardian angel was watching over?"

I'd had no answer for him then, and had nothing further for him weeks later.

The next day being a Monday, the closest thing I got to a day off, Trent and I went to the doctor's, managing to get an appointment mid-morning. I duly peed on a stick and had the pregnancy confirmed. Our baby was going to be due at the beginning of May. I was glad it wasn't April – that would have been far too close to Eva's birthday and would have felt even more as though I was trying to replace her. Although, of course, I hadn't been trying. This had just happened, but it didn't stop me feeling like that.

The doctor – a woman, frizzy redhead, probably early forties, wedding ring, a picture of two gap-toothed grinning children on her desk – asked questions. She had a list of everything to cover and set about it in an organised fashion, but she hadn't looked at my history. The question 'Was this my first pregnancy?' was close to the top, and I saw her pencil hovering over the 'Yes' box.

Trent took my hand as I told her about Eva. She put the pencil down, pushing the efficiency to one side as her bedside manner came out in all its empathy. As we went through the rest of the questions she was kind and thoughtful.

I didn't want to join in with any of the local groups for 'expectant' or 'just had' mums. Those groups had never been my thing anyway, and I didn't want to start explaining my situation to strangers. People always ask "Is this your first?" and I know they'd mean well, but I couldn't answer without it being awkward, both for them and for me. The easiest thing was to answer yes, but it hurt to deny Eva's existence. If I said no then more questions would follow, and I'd seen the frozen expression on people's faces before when they'd found out that I'd had a child, but she'd died. It was much easier to stick to those on the estate who at least knew me, although even there not many knew about Eva. Something else I'd have to face up to.

We left the doctor's and went home. My nausea was already building and I chose to eat cheese and crackers for lunch, wanting something dry and plain. I napped that afternoon, getting the horses in later, and by then I was extraordinarily exhausted, despite the fact I'd done precious little that day. I managed to eat plain boiled pasta for dinner. Trent added a bolognaise sauce to his, which he tried to add to mine as well, but I knew I wouldn't keep it down.

I was the same for the rest of the week, and I knew my feeling as ill as this, coupled with the fact that everyone was going to wonder why Carlton and Greene were doing the riding, meant I was going to have to tell the others on the estate much earlier than I'd anticipated. So the following Monday morning I arrived in the kitchens at the Manor at coffee break time – it was my best opportunity. I'd told Grace and Greene what I was going to do, and both had confirmed they would be there. Trent had asked if I wanted him to go, but I said no. I was hoping only a few would be present so I could tell them, and then the news would disseminate across the estate without me having to say another word.

Mrs F was delighted to see me and hustled me into a seat next to Bray while she poured out coffees for us all. As she pushed a mug across the table I pulled back, knowing if I caught even the slightest aroma of coffee in the steam that rose from the cup it would kick off today's nausea. She looked at me curiously, but I ignored her, then felt a little flustered as I saw Grace raise an eyebrow at me across the table. Greene came over and sat on the other side of me to Bray, giving me a brief smile. Young and Burton were sitting opposite, deep in conversation, but West was away on some radio training course.

Bray asked how I was and I replied quietly that I was fine but I was pretty certain Mrs F and Bray knew something was up.

"We don't often get to see you at this time," she said, trying to continue the conversation, but it felt stilted, like she was probing for information and I knew I needed to get on with spitting out what I'd come to say. I could have asked Grace or Greene to spread the news, but these people were my friends and that felt like the coward's way out. Also no one would have been able to speak to me or ask any questions that way, so I'd thought it had to be done like this.

"No…actually there's something I need to tell you all." I was speaking to Bray, but then cleared my throat and turned to face the others round the table. I repeated, "There's something I need to say," then hesitated, feeling awkward about how to tell them. "Two things, actually…well, Grace and Greene already know…" I floundered, feeling Greene's hand come across and close around my arm, giving me strength. I glanced at her thankfully before finally getting to the point. "But…um…the first is that I'm pregnant."

I heard a little gasp of delight from Bray next to me, and Mrs F's face lit up as her hands covered her mouth.

"Oh, that's wonderful," she enthused, reaching to wrap me in a hug as I stood to receive it, "I'm so thrilled for you." As I pulled back from her I saw her eyes shining with a level of emotion I hadn't expected.

Bray grabbed my attention then as she too hugged me, saying, "I knew there was something going on. Congratulations." The other girls were equally enthusiastic and the questions flowed. When was the baby due? How was I feeling? How long had I known?

Gradually things settled and I pushed my mug of coffee away, no pretence needed now. That was the good part over.

"What's the second thing then?" Burton asked. "Oh, don't tell me the gorgeous Trent has given you twins!"

Everyone laughed, and I grinned as I replied, "Now that thought hadn't crossed my mind and I hope not, but it'll be a few weeks before we have a scan." My smile faded, my head dropped and I clenched my teeth together.

I heard Grace's voice. "Go on," she urged. I could feel the atmosphere around me change as everyone cottoned on to the fact that what was about to follow was not going to be good.

I looked over at her. "I don't want things to change. I don't want everyone to look at me differently." One tear ran down my cheek, which I wiped away.

"They won't, Emma," Greene added. "You're among friends here. We know you and we know you're strong. You can do this."

Bray took my hand. "What is it, love?" I knew she had children, grown up now, off doing their own thing. She would understand, I knew that. But it didn't make it any easier. I took in a deep breath and blew it out slowly. I hadn't thought I'd get so upset again, but it was always the having to say it out loud that got to me.

"Okay." I steadied myself, focusing my gaze for a moment on a dark knot in the scrubbed pine table before looking up and around at those now watching me intently. "I want to tell you all this because I don't want to deny my memories any longer. This will not be my first child. I had a daughter with Alex." My voice cracked as I carried on, "Her name was Eva and she died from an illness when she was six."

"Oh, Emma." Bray wrapped her arms around me, hugging me to her tightly; her shoulder blotted the tears that had run down my face, and when we separated we both wiped our eyes. I was a little embarrassed at the display of emotion and trying to lighten the mood smiled a smile as bright as I could muster. "I'm so sorry for making you all miserable," I said as I looked around the table.

"Don't be, Emma, thank you for telling us," said Mrs F, who had the tissues out. "It's much better we know. It stops us putting our foot in it." She shook her head. "We knew there was something that had brought you great sadness. Do you want to talk about it?" she finished tentatively.

"Not particularly," I shrugged, "but I'm happy to answer any questions." Then as the others drank their coffee we chatted. They asked and I told them about Eva – her life, her death and everything in between.

Eventually I thought it was time I got going so I tried to move things along, "Now you know everything and it has been a tough time, but coming to the estate, meeting all of you and finding Trent has helped me...not to get over it, as such, but to come to terms with it."

24

"We thought it was your divorce." That came from Young and it didn't surprise me. I'd assumed they'd thought that.

"Ah, that was just piled on top." I smiled ruefully.

"Can I ask something…personal…about that?" she continued.

"Of course."

"Did Eva's…did what happened cause the break-up of your marriage?" I noted the pause. People couldn't say it out loud, I'd found that before.

"Indirectly, I guess so." In for a penny, I told myself, they might as well have it all. "I pushed Alex away after Eva died. Although she took after me, I couldn't look at him without seeing her. Everything about him was a reminder: the way he looked at me, his mannerisms. I pushed him away and he had an affair with my best friend. That's what finished our marriage."

I heard the sharp intake of breath around me.

"What a bastard," exclaimed Young.

"What a bitch," chimed in Burton.

"I can't believe they would do that at such a time," Mrs F added crossly. I smiled at their outrage, amazed that I could feel so equable about it now.

"I will never defend her but don't be too hard on him. He was hurting and needed comfort too, and he certainly wasn't getting it from me. But she took advantage and deserves everything she gets." My feelings hadn't changed much there but it felt good standing up for Alex. I'd come a long way on that front. "Look, I don't want to have to keep telling people, so I wondered if you could all let the others know. Just casually, like, when you see them…just those on the estate."

"Of course we will," Bray reassured along with the agreement of the others.

I started to get up to leave, then halted in my tracks as Burton said, "I saw her photo." I looked at her, surprised.

"You did?" I thought I'd been careful about putting it away in the drawer whenever my cottage was due to be cleaned.

She nodded. "Yeah, it was on the bedside cabinet one day. You must have left it out. I wondered who it was. I thought perhaps a niece, but then I thought she looked a lot like you, and I wondered…" She smiled hesitantly, then added abruptly, almost as an afterthought, "I didn't tell anyone."

"Thanks, Kay, I appreciate your discretion."

"Well," said Greene, planting her hands on the table as she made to get up, "if there's one thing we do know all about here, it's discretion," and I laughed along with the others at this understatement as our gathering broke up.

He contemplated the items on the desk in front of him as he sat back in the chair and lifted the glass, the liquid burning its passage down his throat. He didn't need to check in the mirror to know he was pale, he could feel it; an embedded weariness that never lifted palled at him. His very blood was thin, all of him drawn out like the last scrapings of butter across crisp toast. Not surprising really given all that had happened, the decisions he'd had to make.

His hair belied his age, being thick, wavy and still dark, though greying at the temples. No, it was the creases in his face that gave it away; the life he'd led. Each groove was etched by time and emotion into his face as if left there as a marker for every person he'd killed. He didn't need a reminder of any of them; none would be forgotten, so unwillingly had their lives been taken.

He hadn't set out to be what he had become. He remembered a time when he had been proud of his abilities, his talent, not realising then the attention it garnered. How foolish he had been in hindsight. Sometimes, he thought, a person does not choose their

26

career. It chooses them, or someone chooses it for them, as had been the case with him. Now he'd reached the point he'd dreaded. Subconsciously he'd always known it would come one day, but having spent the latter part of his life trying to put it off, trying to do the right thing, it was galling that it was now about to blow up in his face.

Chapter 3

There followed the most miserable few weeks of ill health I'd ever experienced. I woke every morning feeling fine and dandy and able to eat my usual breakfast of toast, but from around noon the day would rapidly deteriorate. Crackers and cheese usually, but not always, stayed down for lunch, but dinner was altogether trickier. The safest bet was plain pasta as long as it wasn't green. I couldn't have anything green on the plate; that would ensure I never ate anything as my stomach heaved just at the sight. Some days even the smell of the food being cooked would be enough to prevent me eating, but generally I managed small amounts of plainly cooked meat, potatoes, rice and a few *non-green* vegetables. At a time when everyone was telling me to eat healthily this was as close to a balanced diet as I could get.

The nausea made life unpleasant, though I tried to keep the truth of how bad I was feeling from Trent, worried he'd stop me working. I'd get the horses ready and tacked up in the morning so Carlton and Greene only had to do the riding. Even though I was struggling, I aimed to get the bulk of my work done in the morning as exhaustion overwhelmed me in the afternoon. I slept every day after lunch and staggered out to do evening stables before collapsing back into the cottage afterwards. I would never have believed anyone could sleep so much.

It was late one afternoon when Carlton caught me being sick by the muck heap. He wrapped me up against his chest and held me tight.

"Don't you think you should take a break now, Em? You're not well and we could easily do more or find someone else to help out."

I pushed him away.

"No, and don't even think of telling Trent about this," I warned. "I am not losing my job."

"Okay." He held his hands up in a placatory manner. "Whatever you want, but you need to take better care of yourself, Em."

"I will, and it will pass," I muttered as I took up the handles of the wheelbarrow and started trundling it back to the yard. "All things do."

The next morning when he and Greene arrived at the yard, Carlton handed me a fancy-looking box of organic ginger tea. He'd done some research, he said, and it was meant to ease morning sickness. Quite overwhelmed he'd gone to the trouble, he looked a little bashful when I told him so, which made me smile.

"You'll make a great father-to-be one day, Carlton." I grinned as he shrugged it off and went to get Regan out, while Greene and I laughed at his discomfort. Carlton and I had always got on, ever since my first day of work here, and there had been a moment when we could have been much more. It would be difficult for anyone not to find him attractive, and I knew he found me so, but that moment had come to nothing other than leaving a connection between us – a bond, if you like – where we cared for each other possibly a little more than was normal.

Greene, fortunately, had no problem with the way we were, and she had turned out to be a great friend to me. Following my experience with my previous friend, Amy, who had slept with my husband, I'd been wary when we first met. Then for a while Greene had ridden out with me and we got to know each other better. I knew she'd come to the estate having come out of a long-term relationship, needing the time to nurse her wounds, and I could relate to that. It wasn't until we were closer friends that she had told me her long-term relationship had been a completely inappropriate one involving a senior officer – a married senior officer. She had known my feelings on women who betrayed other women by taking what wasn't theirs to take, but by the time I knew about this I was much more philosophical about it. I knew it took two, and was actually amazed at her acceptance of the situation she'd found herself in. While he, who should have known better, was still climbing through the ranks to the upper echelons of the Army, she had been advised to leave the role she had carved out for herself, and that must have been a bit of a kicker. I had sympathy for her and the pain that had caused, but what the Army had so foolishly chosen to lose had been the estate's gain. Greene had flourished here, and fallen in love.

Trent was not quite so comfortable with my relationship with Carlton. It had been one of the reasons, along with Alex coming back for me, why at one time he had been possessive of me. To give him his due, though, he had changed. As he had once put it, he aimed to turn his possessiveness into protectiveness, which was better, but I was trying to get him to relax on that front as well. I guess it wasn't surprising he was protective of me considering I'd been attacked by his ex-wife earlier in the summer, then, having practically gone on the run with Grace and the children when the estate came under siege, I had come close to being abducted by Orlov.

When he came into the kitchen at lunchtime and I explained where the ginger tea had come from, I couldn't quite describe the noise he made as he put the box down and wandered through to the sitting room, but it was somewhere between a strangled groan and a growl. However the cup of ginger tea I had with my dry crackers and cheese felt quite soothing and I told him so.

The next day there were three more boxes of it in the cupboard.

We progressed through the rest of what became a blustery October, with the high winds blowing the trees bare and the nights drawing in until all the yard lights had to be turned on for evening stables. There was a brief highlight when Sophia and Reuben came home for half term. I was able to spend some time working with them in the arena, and I tried not to sulk too much when they rode out on a hack with Carlton and Greene instead of me.

Once they had finished with their ponies one day Sophia and Reuben came in to join me for lunch. I loved catching up with them. I'd noticed how much both of them, but particularly Reuben, had grown. I knew by next summer he would have outgrown Benjy and I wondered what Grace and Cavendish wanted to do about that. Moving him on to Zodiac would be the sensible option and then getting something new for Sophia, but I wasn't sure how keen she'd be to relinquish her beloved pony to the tender mercies of her little brother. Problems for another time, I thought.

We sat round the table and while they ate the sandwiches, crisps and fruit I'd doled out to them, I nibbled on some crackers and helped myself to a few of their crisps.

"Why aren't you eating much?" Reuben mumbled through a mouthful of sandwich, gamely trying not to spit bits of it out. They already knew I was pregnant, Grace had told them so they would understand why I wasn't able to ride out with them.

"The baby is making me pretty sick at the moment," I explained, "and don't talk with your mouth full."

"Why is it doing that?" Good question, Reuben, I thought.

"I wish I knew – it's very inconvenient. You know how much I like cake," and I grinned at him as I got up to go and get the cake tin from the side, happy to see his eyes light up.

"Do you know what you're having?" asked Sophia. I shook my head, not wanting to tell them what I was already thinking.

"No, we're saving that as a surprise. There are few enough of those in life."

"Will I be able to look after it?"

"Of course, once Baby is a bit older." I'd had so many offers from people wanting to look after Baby I hoped he, or she, would be good-natured so those offers didn't start being withdrawn.

"Anyway, more importantly, how are you guys getting on back at school?" There had been a decent period of time following 'the incident' during which we had all been busy with wedding plans and then the wedding itself, which had proved a good distraction, but I had often wondered how they were coping once life had returned to normal. The resilience of children is astounding though I knew Cavendish and Grace had arranged some counselling for them.

"Fine," a standard reply from Reuben, whose eyes were firmly fixed on the piece of cake I was now cutting for him, though he then went on to elaborate, "the schoolwork is boring but I've been picked for the football team."

"Congratulations!" I exclaimed, delighted for him as he did love his sport. "You'll have to let me know how you get on." He nodded, munching away happily. Both of them were good at keeping in touch with me by text and I loved hearing their news. "Sophia?" She looked over at me vacantly as if she hadn't even heard the last exchange. "How are you enjoying school?"

"It's okay," she shrugged. I felt saddened. Some of the joy had gone out of her world. I knew she had become anxious and that her parents were worried about her. She liked art and music and I asked her if she would come and play her violin for me sometime but she wasn't that enthusiastic about it. Grace had told me Sophia didn't want to be away at boarding school anymore but they were hoping she'd settle down again as she'd previously loved it there. However if she didn't soon she would be coming home to be enrolled at a local school.

Carlton appeared at the kitchen door asking for volunteers to come and help unload a delivery of hay due to arrive soon. Reuben leapt up, happy to get involved in anything Carlton was doing, and Sophia followed along purely because he encouraged her to. He checked to make sure that everything was all right with me. Then reassured and about to leave he doubled back to tell me Grace had driven into the yard so I asked him to send her in and she could join me for a cup of tea while the children finished off in the barn.

Grace walked in a minute or so later; she'd passed the children so knew what they were up to and as I carried the mugs to the table she asked how I thought Sophia was.

"A bit subdued," I replied, not telling her anything she didn't already know.

"We were thinking we might ask her if she wants us to send someone along as protection when she goes back, if that might make her less anxious." I knew Cavendish and Grace had decided against setting up any sort of additional protection for the children when they went back for the autumn term. Both schools already had a lot of security in place because they attracted the children of many rich and powerful families, any of whom could be potential targets, and Cavendish and Grace hadn't wanted to single their children out. But maybe they needed to revise that.

"I don't know. She hated it last time." And she had. When there had been a kidnap threat against Cavendish,

Young had been despatched to act as her a bodyguard and Sophia had loathed every moment.

"You're right of course." Again I wasn't telling her anything she didn't already know and as Grace fretted about what to do I sympathised, knowing that before too long I would be thrown back into that pit of parenthood where you second guess every decision you make, worrying constantly as to if you're doing the right thing or not.

The following week, when Sophia and Reuben had returned to school, without any additional protection, we passed into the Stygian gloom of November. Although the winds dropped, an extra challenge descended in the form of a murky fog which lifted at best to a fine mist. I could barely see the cottage from the stables most days and the damp air seeped into clothing to add an uncomfortable chill.

Despite Trent's best efforts at pressing food on me, I lost weight. He wasn't happy, the doctor wasn't happy and, to be honest, neither was I, but I was doing my best. If I tried to force the issue, nothing stayed down. As it turned out the baby was doing all right, taking what it needed from me, so it was only my body that was suffering. The draining effects of growing a baby showed in the fragile state of my skin, hair and nails.

The one thing that kept me going through all of this, the one glimmer of hope for me, was that this pregnancy was nothing like the one I'd experienced with Eva. With her I'd been traditionally sick a couple of mornings, a little weary a few evenings, and that was it. And it was this that focused my mind on the fact that this baby was going to be a boy. Although we chose not to find out when we went for the scan, I told Trent of my suspicions and ignored the sceptical look that came across his face. He tentatively suggested we should keep an open mind and that we should discuss girls' names as well as those for boys, but I would have none of it. With my mind made up, I blanked out Trent's worries and imagined the boy that was coming – the boy that wouldn't be a replacement for Eva.

Trent's delight at seeing our baby on the scan was wonderful to experience. He proudly took the grainy photo everywhere, whipping it out to show everyone he came across. This was a happy interlude in a bleak time when he was away quite a bit with Cavendish, taking Carlton and Wade with them. Greene had her work cut out with the horses, though Grace stepped in to fill the breach where she could, and we muddled through.

Trent didn't say much about his work away. He wasn't meant to – even though we'd all signed non-disclosure agreements, his work, being with the Secret Intelligence Service, was of a higher level altogether. I remembered a conversation I'd once had with Grace when she'd said, "They can't tell you what they've been through and you learn not to ask", but Trent and I had built up a sort of code so I had a rough idea of what was going on. If he told me he was 'off for a couple of days', even if it was longer than that, I'd know he was staying on home soil. If he was 'going for a while', he was overseas.

He was 'going for a while' more and more often now and that worried me. He, Cavendish and the others were working to bring the Polzin organisation down, and as well as it being a dangerous job it was also an endless battle and, as Trent and I had discussed, it wasn't as if bringing them down would be the end of anything anyway. There would always be another scummy organisation waiting to fill the gap should one arise. But they had to tackle what was in front of them, and in this case the heads of the Polzin family needed to be taken out to stand any chance of the organisation crumbling. That was proving hard to achieve. The senior Polzin brothers kept themselves behind the scenes; it was only the youngest, Anatoly, who took an active role in the business. Being visible made him the easiest target, but since the attack on the estate he had gone into hiding – both him and his right-hand man, Orlov, and it was Orlov I wanted put away.

I knew no progress had been made against those two whenever Trent returned. I only had to look at him to receive the subtlest shake of the head. No words were needed. He knew the news I was after.

However, what I did know was as well as trying to get close to the leaders of the Polzin family they set out to cause as much devastation to the organisation as they could along the way. It was the trouble they'd caused previously that had brought Anatoly and Orlov out of the woodwork before and it was hoped it would have the same effect again.

Two things happened to brighten our lives a week or so before Christmas. The first was Turner's return to the estate. He'd been gone since just after our wedding, having booked himself into a residential centre for some intensive psychotherapy to help him recover from 'the incident'. During the attack Anatoly and his men had abducted him off the estate, badly beaten him, and used him to get their troops onto the estate and to take a plane from RAF Loreley. Turner had been humiliated, but even worse than the beating had been the fact that he thought he'd let everyone down, though there wasn't anything he could have done about it. It had changed him. From being the light-hearted boy I'd known since I'd come to the estate, he'd become angry, brooding and withdrawn. He'd started to spend more and more time at the gym, and hanging out around the stables. It had been this that had first raised Trent's concerns, but the catalyst for the extended trip away had been the night he'd attacked me when we were sparring at kickboxing. It had been my fault: I'd goaded him, pushed every button until he exploded, and I felt guilty for what I had so stupidly done.

My heart lifted, though, the morning I looked up from my mucking out to see him approach the post-and-rail fence that ran round the yard. I kept my face neutral, not sure how he'd be.

He stopped at the open stable door, his breath misting on the cold morning air, and planted his hands deep in his jeans pockets as he lifted his chin. "Hey."

I leaned on my fork as I took a breather.

"Hey yourself." I studied him for a moment. He'd filled out – hours at the gym, I guessed – and he looked older, more like the other boys on the estate; more experienced, less filled with the exuberance of youth and innocence. "How're you doing, Turner?"

"Pretty good, and you?"

I lifted my hand and tilted it from side to side. "So-so."

"I hear congratulations are in order."

"Thanks." Good to hear the estate telegraph was spreading the word.

"You look tired, Grayson, and too thin." Nothing like getting straight to it.

"Yeah, I've not been feeling too great."

"Sorry, that was clumsy of me. I heard you'd been having a rough time. Can I give you a hand?" I shrugged. I wasn't sure that was a good idea.

"I don't know, Turner, is it okay you being here?"

He shrugged and grinned. "I've been given the all-clear and told it's absolutely fine for me to be here." Somehow I doubted that, but I smiled as I handed him the fork, all help being much appreciated, and went to get on with the next stable.

We finished a while later and as the horses hadn't come back from exercise yet I offered him a coffee and we wandered over to the cottage. It briefly crossed my mind as we went into the kitchen if it was a good idea, but by then I was committed and could hardly change my mind

37

without coming up with a good reason, which I didn't have – and anyway I felt perfectly comfortable in his presence.

He asked after Susie and I told him she was fine and out on the ride with Carlton and Greene. He seemed relaxed as he sat at the kitchen table and I pushed the biscuit tin across the table, telling him to help himself.

"You look good, Turner – working out as hard as ever I take it."

"Thanks, yeah it's all part of my anger management."

"Oh right." I remembered Trent telling me he had been through the same thing. Using exercise to dispel the anger he felt. He'd made me laugh when he told me that some days all he did was exercise. He'd mellowed since and I hoped Turner would eventually too. As I passed him his coffee he surprised me.

"Do you feel okay with me being here, Emma? Do you feel safe?" He looked unsettled for a moment, awkward and embarrassed. Distracted briefly by seeing the horses arriving in the yard I glanced back at him.

"Yeah, I do, Turner, I feel completely okay with it," and I smiled, pleased to see him respond with a grin. It was good to have him back.

The second thing that made our lives considerably brighter was that I stopped suffering from morning sickness. One day I was bad, and the next I got to lunchtime and suddenly realised the nausea hadn't kicked in. I ate my crackers and cheese as usual, not wanting to tempt fate, and they settled in my stomach without any problems. I even felt less tired that afternoon, and by dinnertime I was still awake. Dinner that evening tasted like normal food again – no odd metallic tastes, no weird smells putting me off – and I even managed some green stuff.

Mrs F had sent two cherry tarts home with Trent. She had been relentless in her sending of provisions ever since I'd broken the news, but most of them had gone into Trent.

I'd thanked her and let her know the situation, but she hadn't given up, forever hopeful. Now that resilience of hers was repaid. I eyed the tarts hungrily and wolfed mine down before Trent had even made a start on his. With a smile he slid his tart over onto my plate. I made a half-hearted objection before demolishing it and was still clearing my mouth as I looked over at him.

"God, that was good. What a relief. Though you can't keep passing your food over to me, I'll end up huge."

"I think you can cope with it for the time being, Em. You're nearly five months pregnant and you can hardly tell." He was right: my stomach was barely rounded between hips that were too prominent.

I found more of the tarts in the fridge the next day, and the next, and the next, and they never lasted long. I supposed it was a craving of sorts, or my body needing to make up for lost time.

While enjoying a decent meal at last was wonderful, the best part of that evening, the very best part, was getting to go to bed at the same time as my husband. I curled into him, feeling his warmth radiate into my body. His arm went around me as he held me close.

"How are you feeling, Em?"

"Terrific. I think it's finally over." I could feel myself smiling with the relief.

"So...you're up for some fun?"

"Absolutely." The word breathed against lips which brushed mine softly, tenderly, the gentlest touch of his tongue on mine all that was required to make me hot and needy. His hands travelled their way across my body, his lips caressing my skin, his tongue leaving a trail of fire in its wake. Desire grew as he teased his way down my neck, across my shoulders, lingering on my breasts, tasting, touching and sucking on nipples that begged for attention. It had been a while, a long while. The romantic side of our life had suffered while I'd felt so ill and although I'd kept him satisfied with early-morning sex, it hadn't been nearly enough.

Now my body cried out for him, my hips rising as I willingly succumbed to the pleasure he gave me and which built rapidly. I longed for release, yet skilfully he held me as if in suspension, every sensation heightened by his constant attention. Desperate to be pushed over the edge I called out, breathless and grasping his hands as with a final flick I came, crashing over hard and fast, the quick blinding intensity that rolled through my body exquisitely prolonged by his unrelenting tongue until I could bear it no longer and I pushed him away.

He reared up over me then, soft skin over the solid muscle of his chest, his stomach, and I reached for him, pulling him down towards me, my fingers pushing roughly into his hair, feeling him, hard against still tender flesh that made me gasp as he drove into me, thrusting deeply, his lips coming down passionately on mine as he powered into me over and over until suddenly he tensed tight up against me, groaning loudly, his body shuddering until finally he collapsed, heavy and breathing hard. Eventually he rolled off me and we lay fully sated and wordless, falling asleep in a tangle of bodies and sheets.

I woke the next morning with a smile on my face and, cheesy though it may be, a song in my heart as I hummed my way downstairs.

"Someone's got their bounce back." He grinned as I popped bread in the toaster before wrapping my arms around him. He'd told me the previous evening he was going to be 'off for a couple of days' and he was wearing his holster under his left arm. His gun lay on the table, an indicator of the state of alert on the estate. Since the attack all who were licensed to carry did. While it remained our intention to take down the Polzin organisation, it was likely that at some point they would retaliate against us. It made me edgy, his holster, always there as a reminder of the situation we were in, but I thought it was interesting how I now thought of the estate as 'we'. It was the estate and everyone on it instead of only Trent and Cavendish against the bad guys. Maybe I was more of a team player than I'd thought.

He drained his glass before placing it back on the desk and turned his attention to the pile of photographs he had in front of him. Leaving the top one to the side, he looked carefully through the others, as he had done whenever he'd had the opportunity. He savoured each one as he took his time, gazing at them, allowing the memories each evoked to flood back in. It was highly likely he would never see them again.

He checked they were in order then placed them back on the desk, returning to the one he'd previously put aside. He'd recently received it from his clients. Their instructions always followed the same pattern: a photo would be given to him which would show his next target. In this case, more correctly, targets.

The photo featured two men and two women standing on the steps of a courthouse. He knew where it was. A red cross had been drawn, using a permanent marker, over the hearts of each of the two men and one of the women. The other woman, it appeared, was of no importance in the plans of his clients.

One of the crosses had a circle around it.

It was this circle that made all the difference.

It was this circle that had shown that this was not business.

This was personal.

And he didn't like that. He didn't like that one bit.

Chapter 4

Now I was no longer spending my days feeling debilitated by nausea I was looking forward to spending Christmas at the Manor. Cavendish and Grace were hosting an open house again. As Turner settled back into life on the estate he was occasionally free and he 'volunteered' to come and help out at the stables. I guessed this was at Trent's instigation, part of his less than subtle plan to introduce more assistance gradually for me at the stables, as if I wouldn't notice. However, I was particularly pleased to make use of the extra help on Christmas Eve. Because I wasn't riding and because I had Turner's help I got the stables done in double-quick time, which meant I could fit in a visit to Eva.

I placed the flowers in the vase buried in the black granite, this time a warm and comforting array of reds and ambers, and I remembered the icy white roses I'd brought in error the previous year. I was pleased to see a small wreath already on the grave. It was pretty: red berries interwoven with a richly coloured tartan ribbon. I imagined Alex laying it there for her and hoped he was moving on.

I sat on the bench, filled her in on life on the estate and told her about the baby. I had no doubt she already knew – my dreams showed me that, but this made it official and I couldn't help but hope she was okay with it; that she understood. I told her we were starting to get the nursery ready. It would be decorated in greens and yellows, neutral, nothing stereotypical. Trent's suggestion, which had made me laugh. Eva had insisted from almost as soon as she could talk that she wanted her room to be blue and we'd covered the cream with paint the colour of robin's eggs, softened with a cornflower blue that I believed matched her eyes.

I let her know I thought it was a boy, a blond-haired boy. Trent had once told me he had been blond as a child, his hair only darkening to a rich dark brown as he grew up, and since then I'd thought of my boy: blond, blue-eyed and solemn. I didn't know why solemn, but I couldn't imagine having a giggly baby. Perhaps because Trent had always been so serious, I saw his son as a smaller version of the same.

Trent had changed. If not with the outside world, where I was sure he was still the same hard man life had made him, then at least with me. After years of living in sad loneliness he felt secure and loved, and by giving him everything I had I found myself in the privileged position of being allowed to see through the tough exterior to the softer soul inside. To my surprise I discovered that I was the centre of his existence. I had never been that to anyone, not even Alex, and it was both overwhelming and deeply touching.

I hoped he felt I was as open as he was about my feelings, but I wasn't sure and I didn't know how to bare my soul in the way he did to me. We weren't needy people, never feeling like we had to keep telling the other we loved them. That was a given; once said it was meant forever, but sometimes I wondered if I should say more, tell him how much he meant to me. I just didn't know how.

I stayed with Eva for a while, trying to think back to what life had been like when she had been a baby. That had been more than ten years ago now, a lifetime, and a time when I was an entirely different person. Eventually I left, promising as always I'd be back.

I returned to the cottage late afternoon, delighted to find Trent's truck parked in the yard showing he'd made it

43

home for Christmas. He'd been 'off for a couple of days'. I made a fuss of Susie as she scampered out to greet me. Like the previous year, a beautifully decorated tree had magically appeared in the cottage and was lit by the glow from the lights that adorned it as well as a golden warmth coming from the wood burner.

I found Trent asleep on the settee. Music played softly in the background and I sat on the other one and watched him for a while.

He was a man who worried too much, and although he had much to worry about with things as they were, he did overburden himself, taking on more than his fair share of the load. I loved watching him sleep; it was then I got to see his face truly relaxed. The warm light highlighted angled planes and softened others with shadows cast. His jawline was dark with stubble; his hair lay across his forehead, reaching down to beautifully curved brows above thickly lashed eyes. Lips, soft in repose, tempted me and I moved closer to kiss them; my sleeping beauty stirred and woke in our role reversal. He smiled sleepily as he reached his arms around me.

"Hi," he murmured.

"Hi." I kissed him again, firmer this time, and felt him take notice as his arms tightened their hold. I pulled away to look at him. "I'm off to do evening stables, be back in a bit."

"Don't go." His eyes were barely open. "I have plans to get you into bed." I chuckled; while his heart might be willing I was pretty sure his flesh would not be that interested. Whenever he returned he needed recovery time – cuts and bruises had to be treated and the sleep of the dead slept – but it never failed to amaze me how quickly he bounced back.

"Work now, play later," I whispered against his lips as I quickly kissed him goodbye before unwrapping his arms from my body and leaving him to drift back off into sleep, which he looked like he could use.

We woke early on Christmas Day, pulled on thick coats to go and feed Susie and the horses then went back to bed where we snuggled up and swapped presents. I had struggled to come up with a gift for Trent, settling eventually for silver cufflinks; not exactly original, but he liked them. He gave me a beautiful silver locket, an antique. It contained a photo of Eva, the other side left blank for Baby.

I sat up to allow Trent to put it on me and once he had he reached down to the hem of my vest top and pulled it up and over my head. I raised one eyebrow in question and he grinned salaciously.

"I want to see you wearing only this." Always happy to oblige I wriggled out of my lounge pants as he stripped and pulled me close. He was hungry. I could feel it in his kisses, in the urgency of his restless body. Usually we took our time, revelling in the enjoyment of each other, but this was not one of those occasions. A cobweb-shaking session of raw, animalistic passion worked just as effectively and falling back on the pillows panting and laughing with him a short time later I couldn't help thinking how much my Christmases had improved since I'd come to the estate.

We enjoyed a fabulous feast at the Manor. Most of our friends, or at least those who didn't have family elsewhere, were with us, and encouraged by how much I ate from then on Trent tried to feed me at every opportunity. He was keen for me to gain some weight which was fair enough, but I didn't want it to get out of hand so I insisted on starting back at the gym, which I hadn't been to since the morning sickness first struck. Cavendish brought in a fitness trainer to work out a suitably modified routine for me and I was back to fitting my workout in at the end of each day when I'd finished at the stables. I started to look and feel much healthier. My skin glowed, my hair was glossy and I was full of energy. Trent and I started socialising with the others again, enjoying pub nights at The Red Calf, though being the designated driver every time wasn't quite as much fun.

My enjoyment of food wasn't the only appetite that was fully restored, and over the next couple of months barely a night passed, if Trent was at home, when I didn't get to indulge in my reawakened passion for him. He was never one to say no, but unfortunately for him, and for reasons unknown to me, my libido peaked in the early hours. It would wake me up and, knowing I'd never get back to sleep again, I'd reach for him. I knew it was selfish to wake him, but I banked on the fact he'd always come round to my way of thinking. I'd snuggle up, my body pressing against his warm skin, and wrap my leg across his, running my hand over his chest, brushing my fingers through the light covering of dark hair then caressing slowly downwards, following the trail as it tapered away across the flat muscle of his stomach. Generally by then I'd have gained his full attention and like he'd awoken in the middle of an erotic dream he'd become an active participant in our lovemaking. If not I worked on him more, using my hands, my lips, my mouth...He loved that – there was *no* ignoring that. Just as he, and I, loved my nipples brushing through his chest hair as he held me close, hungrily searching for my mouth as I moved over him, his hips driving against me in rhythm as we sought our mutual goal. Then, satisfaction achieved, we'd collapse, hot and panting, unravelling from one another to drift back into the folds of sleep.

I realised the toll this was taking on him when I came in from the gym on several occasions to find him fast asleep in the sitting room. I'd get dinner on, or progress what he'd already started, and he'd wake, appearing in the door to the kitchen, stretching and yawning as he rubbed his eyes.

"God, woman, you're wearing me out," he'd mumble into my neck as I hugged him to me, feeling the stirrings of desire as I did. I loved my new levels of energy almost as much as Trent loved what was happening to my body. He enjoyed every change as I gradually filled out, and while I could understand his increased interest as my breasts got larger, I was surprised by how delighted he was as my stomach grew.

We were lying on the settee one evening, comfortably relaxed and settled with Trent's hand resting on my bump, when he felt Baby move for the first time. I'd been feeling it for a while now, right from the fluttering butterfly movements as I'd been sitting eating dinner one evening to the now more obvious stretches and kicks. Several times I'd grabbed Trent's hand and pressed it to my stomach, but there had been no more movements, as if Baby had had a sudden bout of shyness. This time, though, it made him jump. He kept his hand in place, hoping for more, and stared in fascination as he watched a ripple move under my skin as Baby went for a walk.

"That is amazing," he stated, pointing at my bump and I laughed at his astonishment at something I was learning to live with. "Does it hurt?"

"Not really...it's usually stretches and wiggles I feel rather than kicks, though they'll get stronger as Baby gets bigger. I remember one time when I was expecting Eva I actually saw an outline of a foot as she kicked me when I was in the bath."

"Oh, that's weird," he replied, a worried frown appearing on his face.

"You'd think it would be, but then when it happens it feels normal."

He was quiet for a moment then cleared his throat. "Er...I was wondering if we should discuss some baby names." I'd known this was coming, that he'd been sensing when I'd be most receptive, and over the last few days I'd already had a couple of gentle hints. "Charlotte's a nice name," he'd mentioned most recently while reading the paper, no doubt while taking in an article about a notable Charlotte. I'd made some sort of noncommittal noise and moved on.

He'd already made it crystal clear he wanted traditional names. Names that wouldn't stand out, that wouldn't earn Baby a beating at school. I thought this was a shame as, having lived with the quite ordinary Emma, I liked his Ezekiel better and quite fancied the idea of something a little more flamboyant, but any suggestions I'd made in the past had been shot down in flames.

"We haven't discussed any girls' names, Emma." Though he'd come straight to the point, I could feel him testing the water to see if I was any closer to coming round to his way of thinking, which was to keep an open mind.

"There's no need to," I replied, probably a little more bluntly than I meant to.

"Emma…" his reasoning tone.

"If it comes to it, Trent, we'll come up with something then. But I honestly don't think there's any need."

"Okay." He sighed, then after a moment of quiet moved on. "Boys' names then. What about William Henry? What do you think?"

I thought, as names went, they were pretty safe actually, and more than a little unoriginal considering they belonged to the two men we were closest to. William Henry Trent. Hmm. Will Trent. I liked the sound of that.

I was still thinking when he added, "They might make good godfathers too." This was new and I hadn't thought that far ahead, but yes, they seemed to be the obvious people to ask. It wasn't as if either of us had brothers who would fill that role.

"Yeah…I like that idea." It pleased me that he was thinking of Carlton like that. "But as we're not religious, would we go down the route of having a christening?"

"Ahh, I see what you mean, and you're right, we wouldn't, but I think we should have people in place in the roles of godparents. Our four closest friends would be ideal."

"Yes, they would, and I like the name, as long as we can shorten it to Will…if it suits him."

Trent tilted his head as he considered. "I'm happy with that. It's a good, strong name and he'll blend in when he goes off to boarding school."

I didn't hesitate. Not for a second.

"That won't be happening." It was a statement, and as far as I was concerned a final one. I didn't even break stride making it.

"I know it's a long way off, but surely he'll go to the same school I did?" He looked puzzled.

"Our son will not be going away to school."

"Why not?" he queried as I pushed myself up into a sitting position.

"I will not be separated from another child, Trent, ever, and certainly not because of some old boys' tradition. Our child can go to the local school. It's a perfectly good school and he will come home each day. We will be the ones who bring him up and make him into the man he will become, not some school miles away where we have no idea what is happening in his life and we end up with a stranger coming home to us for the odd weekend." I knew I was being a little unfair, but I also wanted to draw my line in the sand and this was one point on which I was not going to budge.

"It's not really like that," he argued weakly.

"I will not be separated from him." The 'and that is final' bit was implied by my tone and I didn't feel the need to add it.

The winter was turning out to be an icy one and though the cold could be biting it was easier to work in than when it was wet and miserable. White sparkling mornings greeted me with breaths blown out in frosted clouds and frosts so thick they crunched beneath my boots as I crossed to the yard each day.

With my growth spurt I eventually had to concede I needed new clothes so went on a shopping trip to stock up. Fortunately we had no big events coming up that I might need some sort of dress for as frankly they were all hideous, so I was able to get an assortment of jeans and tops that I thought would see me through. As I wandered along the high street of the town I stopped outside the window of a baby store. I'd left Trent that morning tackling the painting of the nursery and I wondered if I should buy anything for it. I started towards the door, then hesitated. It felt like it was tempting fate to buy things for a baby before its safe arrival and I didn't need anything jinxing Baby's future. I walked away, headed back to the car and drove home.

When I got back Trent had been busy. Susie was keen to let me know something was going on upstairs when I greeted her, and as I carried my purchases up to our bedroom I paused on the landing to watch Trent hard at work. Sticking with the original plan, two walls were going to be green and two yellow; pale pastels, the soothing colours of nature. We'd discussed getting in some of the others to help, but he'd said it was something he wanted to do, and so far he'd finished the green. He grinned as he showed off his handiwork proudly and I smiled at the splashes of paint that decorated him. He looked relaxed and carefree; one of those moments to cherish at a time when such opportunities didn't present themselves that often.

By the end of the next day the nursery was finished, but empty. We stood looking round it and I knew we needed to get some stuff ahead of the game. I explained my aborted trip to the baby shop to Trent.

"One step at a time," he reminded me. "We'll go together and get the furniture and the basics, but nothing personal until Baby arrives," and thus reassured I nodded.

"When shall we go?" I was feeling much more positive about it now he was going to be with me.

"Tomorrow…" and he turned away, busying himself with clearing up the dust sheets. It was in that one word that I knew he was leaving again.

Trent was quite right in his advice to take things one step at a time. This philosophy was working well on dealing with the baby stuff and I had other, more concerning things to focus on. Trent was often away now, telling me he was 'going for a while' and my mind was occupied more and more with worries for his safety. It was the same for many on the estate, and those of us left behind spent quite a few of our evenings socialising. Although security on the estate was heightened, we made an effort to meet at The Red Calf, generally once a week, varying our nights, trying to ensure we did nothing in a pattern at a time when any interested parties might view the estate as vulnerable. Not that it was: a skeleton staff was always on duty and vigilance was maintained on the estate cameras.

Grace spent a good deal of her time making sure everyone was keeping their spirits up and organising various little gatherings, occasionally outings. We would rotate meeting up at each other's places, and numbers attending fluctuated depending on unavoidable work commitments.

I knew that everyone was keeping a particularly close eye on me and I appreciated the support. While I enjoyed having time to myself and generally only having the company of Susie and the horses during the day, the evenings could be tiresomely long and filled with concerns for Trent, the others on the estate and, inevitably, the baby. I longed to know what Trent was up to, but contact was intermittent and, whereas he could ask me things about my life, I couldn't reciprocate. It was frustrating. Others on the estate were in exactly the same situation and understood completely.

One of the people who straddled both worlds was Greene. Sometimes she went away with them, sometimes she was left behind, and it was on one occasion when she and Grace had popped round to mine that she opened up in a way she hadn't before. They were sharing a bottle of wine and Grace was updating me with news of the children. I was looking forward to spending some time with Sophia and Reuben over the upcoming holidays and also to afterwards, when the baby had arrived and I could get back to riding out with them. As it was I had plans to increase the amount of jumping we did in the arena and paddocks, which I was sure they would love. Greene had been listening quietly, and casually added into the conversation that she and Carlton had discussed starting a family. She paused, then asked us what we thought.

"It will change your life," I stated, keeping my tone neutral. I glanced at Grace who inclined her head in support of my statement, then reached over to refill Greene's glass.

"I know," Greene sipped her wine. "There'll be no more taking off at a moment's notice on exciting missions or, I guess, spontaneity of any kind." And while I nodded in agreement, that's not what I'd meant at all.

I wanted her to know what none of us can possibly know before we venture down the precarious path of parenthood. I wanted her to know the one thing that no one can tell you, that no book will reveal, which is that while the physical wounds of childbirth heal, becoming a mother leaves an emotional wound so raw that she would be forever vulnerable.

I considered warning her that if accidents, diseases or famines were reported in the news they would haunt her, and she would wonder if anything could be worse than watching her child die. And I could assure her that nothing would even come close, and I knew that she would nod sympathetically yet still have no idea what I really meant.

Greene was an attractive woman. She worked hard on maintaining her physique and I wanted to tell her she would eventually lose the weight she would put on during pregnancy, but she would never feel the same about herself again. Her life, which was now so important, would be of less value to her once she had a child, and she would give it up in an instant to save her offspring. At the same time she would long for more years, not for fulfilling her own dreams, but to see her child accomplish theirs.

I wanted to describe to her the exhilaration of seeing her child learn to ride a bike, or what it was like to hear the belly laugh of a baby when it made some brand new and exciting discovery.

I wanted her to taste the joy that was so real it hurt.

I realised Greene was looking at me in a rather strange way and that tears had formed in my eyes. I looked over at Grace again and we grinned at each other. I knew she was with me and I raised my glass of elderflower cordial to theirs of wine.

Almost as one, Grace and I said, "You'll never regret it."

Most of the time, when Trent was away I went to the various doctor's appointments and check-ups alone, which I was happy to do, but he happened to be at home when we eventually had a brief tour round the local hospital's maternity unit at the beginning of March. This made him appreciate just how quickly the birth was approaching.

After he spent a good part of the next day timing how long it would take him to get to the hospital via a couple of different routes, I had a sobering moment when I found this information typed up. We didn't live the kind of lives that could be put on hold. Trent could be anywhere when I went into labour and could hardly ask in the middle of a mission God only knew where if it was all right to pop home and attend the birth. I realised he was planning for the fact that he might not be there. We hadn't spoken about it, but I was a practical person and knew it might well be someone else driving me.

When Trent went away Cavendish always went with him, but more and more often they took others too. Therefore I could never rely on Carlton, Hayes or Wade being around, although I noticed Turner had not yet been taken back out into the field. Trent and I had discussed this and he had told me it was too soon to risk Turner coming up against Anatoly. They were concerned that Turner's need for personal vengeance would override any thoughts of his own safety or that of others with him, and they needed to know he'd put the success of the mission before exorcising any demons of his own.

With these thoughts in mind I made my own backup plan. I waited until Greene and Grace arrived one morning to ride and asked them if they would be willing to take me to the maternity unit and be with me, should the worst happen and Trent wasn't there for the birth. Both said yes, though Greene's agreement was obviously on the proviso she was around and I was relieved to have my team, or at least part of it in the form of Grace, definitely in place.

When I'd finished the stables that morning I went up to the Manor to give what, since Christmas, had become a weekly briefing on my condition to those who turned up for morning coffee. Many were taking a keen and seemingly genuine interest in the impending arrival of Baby, so I reciprocated by being more sociable when I could be and imparting information whenever I had some to share. On this morning there was only Mrs F and Bray present, and we sat chatting about inconsequential things for a few minutes before Bray excused herself as she had to get on. As she left, the door slamming behind her, the baby kicked out obviously which drew Mrs F's attention to my stomach.

She looked a little uncomfortable as she asked, "Emma, would you mind if I?" and made a movement with her hand in the direction of my stomach.

"Oh, of course not, go ahead." As she placed her hand on me I moved it to the place where I could feel Baby turning, and sure enough, moments later, there was a violent wiggle followed by a kick. Mrs F gasped.

"Oh my goodness, that's incredible." She took her hand away, and as she met my eyes I saw the tears in hers.

Alarmed, I placed a hand on her arm. "I'm sorry, I didn't mean for you to get upset." She shook her head, blinking the tears away.

"You haven't. It's amazing, and I'm so happy for you. It's just one of those things I wish I'd got to experience."

I didn't know much about her past, so asked hesitantly, "Did you try...to have children?"

"We did. Technically I guess we've never given up trying..." and she laughed, though it sounded bittersweet. "But we were already too old when we got together, and it's never happened for us."

"I'm sorry." It sounded inadequate against such sadness, but she patted my hand and gave me a big smile.

"Such are life's disappointments, Emma. We all have our crosses to bear, you know that more than most, and as long as I get plenty of baby cuddles and am called on for babysitting duties I shall be perfectly happy."

I beamed at her. "You can count on it."

It was the third week of March. Trent had got back the previous evening, his mood darkened with exhaustion having been away for nearly two weeks. He'd slept, spent the morning at the Manor, and had just driven back into the yard. I knew before he even got out of the truck he was leaving again. He sat there watching me, deep in thought, and I just knew.

I closed Regan's door and wandered across to where he'd parked. He was still sitting there, and it wasn't until I opened the door that he moved at all. He turned to me; not a word.

"You're going again, aren't you?" I didn't need to wait for an answer. "You've only just got back, Trent, you're knackered." I was stating the obvious for something to say more than anything else and didn't expect a response. He only shrugged. "What?" I continued. "You seem strange, distracted."

He spoke, still deep in thought. "Yeah...it's probably nothing, but we've been ordered to go to headquarters, which is a bit unusual." He seemed to be wracking his brains as to the reason, then made a move to get out of the cab. "I've just got a feeling that something's not right and I can't quite put my finger on what it is."

"What does Cavendish think?"

"I'm not sure. We haven't had a chance to talk – we've only just received the order and are reacting to it, but I think he thinks like me."

"Maybe it's for a meeting of some sort, or to pass on some intel," I volunteered.

"Maybe, but if it was intel they would just pass it on. They wouldn't need to meet with us." Although he didn't seem convinced, he suddenly brightened a little. "I guess if it is just a meeting, though, I'll be back very soon." Checking his watch, he finished, "I've just got time for a shower, then we're off."

"Okay, I'll go and carry on and see you before you go," and I watched him walk to the cottage before I turned back to the stables.

He was ready within ten minutes and came over to give me a hug, all wet hair and smelling clean and soapy. He placed one hand on my stomach. "All quiet?"

"Yes, Baby's enjoying a mid-morning nap, saving its energy to give me a good kicking later." I smiled and he withdrew his hand, reluctantly.

"Look after both of you, Em," and he kissed me, deliciously minty fresh.

"Of course," I replied as the kiss ended.

He groaned. "I don't want to go."

I pushed at him playfully. "Go on, get it over with and get back here."

"Okay, I won't be long," and I watched as he walked away.

With no idea how wrong he was…

Two weeks earlier…

The receipt of this photo had changed everything for him. Every decision he now took, every plan he now made was because of this. The ridiculous thing was that, even after all the precautions he'd taken, they'd still arrived at this point, though this turn of events had not been of his making, which had surprised him. He'd always thought that it would be because of something he did that this die would be cast, but as it had turned out he'd ended up in this position even though his clients still remained oblivious as to what – or whom – they were dealing with. This made it all the more precarious because he wanted that situation to remain the same for as long as possible. Timing was everything now. Picking up a pen, he flipped the photo over and made his mark on the back.

He reached across the desk to pull a wooden box towards him, then placed all the photos inside before closing it carefully. He ran his fingers lightly across the warmth of the golden wood, hoping, wishing he could impart a memory, then he wrapped it in plain brown paper and addressed it, although this was one parcel he would not be trusting to any courier. He would deliver it himself.

He sat back after filling his glass again and contemplated what he'd done, the plans he'd put in place, going over every detail to ensure, with his usual dedication and attention, he'd not missed anything. There'd be no room for mistakes. He knew after he'd delivered this parcel there would be no going back and the card he was throwing down in the deadly game he now played marked the beginning of what he had come to realise would be his end.

Chapter 5

My impatience for him to return was a little out of character. Normally I relished a bit of time on my own, but it was unusual nowadays for Trent not to give me any indication of when he would return. A call or a text would not have gone amiss, I thought grumpily as I washed up after a light supper of chicken and salad. At least with Trent away I didn't have him complaining about how little I was eating. He didn't understand that with Baby now being the size he was there was little room for anything else; he still felt the need to feed me at any opportunity, afraid I would fade away when it was patently obvious there was precious little chance of that happening for a good while yet.

I put my unsettled state down to the nature of his call into work. He didn't often get ordered to go to headquarters, especially when he'd only recently got back; he usually just received details of wherever he was needed and because of that peculiarity I was curious as to what it was about. I had hoped it was positive and that there was news on the whereabouts of Anatoly and Orlov, but the call had made me edgy. Call it my sixth sense, but I couldn't help thinking that for some reason he, and presumably Cavendish, were in trouble. This was mainly due to the fact they had gone to that meeting on Friday – it was now Sunday.

And there had been no contact.

Wandering into the sitting room I thought I might watch a film, but after running my finger along the spines of the DVDs on the shelf looking for inspiration, I found none. So I curled up on the settee and picked up my book instead. Susie joined me, wriggling up as close as possible and after winding herself into a ball, she promptly fell asleep.

I started reading, my hand resting on my belly, feeling the movements coming from Baby. True to form, the minute I was still the kicking and stretching from within began. I had a feeling we were going to have a light sleeper on our hands.

So deep was I in my book that I jumped when my phone went. Trent's ringtone broke the silence previously only punctuated by Susie's light snoring and her occasional whimpering as she dreamt of chasing prey.

"Hello," I answered, eager to have the chance to find out what he was up to.

"Good evening, Grayson," came the response. Okaaay, I thought, taken aback – that was a little formal. I could feel the frown form on my face.

"Good evening to you too," I replied carefully, knowing he would feel the unease in my words. "What's going on, Trent?"

"Carlton's on his way to pick you up." His tone was brusque and jangling bells rang as questions formed.

"What's going on?" I repeated quickly, my voice sharper this time.

"I can't tell you."

"Why aren't you picking me up?" For that matter, why couldn't I drive myself?

"I'm not allowed to…" and he ended the call. His voice was matter of fact, as if it was not me he was talking to. Why would that be? I didn't understand and my mind went into overdrive. After no contact at all he called and talked to me like that? No affection, no warmth, no information. It was as if he was annoyed at me for something, but I couldn't think what that could be.

Or – I thought rapidly – it was that he was unable to speak freely. Ahh, that was it! Someone was with him, preventing him from saying more. But who could it be? Someone here on the estate? I dismissed that as unlikely; it wouldn't make him unfriendly towards me.

Someone who had come onto the estate? A sudden wave of anxiety passed through me. Were we being attacked again? No, don't be ridiculous, I told myself, he wouldn't have rung me like that if we were. There would be an estate-wide warning and he wouldn't have informed me Carlton was coming to get me. No, it wasn't that. I shook my head, frustrated with not knowing what was going on.

His attitude had definitely been off, and what was that about him not being *allowed* to come and get me? That was odd. There was only one thing I was sure of: he was giving me a warning. I didn't know what for, but I knew I needed to be on my guard.

I was interrupted from my train of thought by a quick rapping on the back door which opened to reveal Carlton. I'd been so distracted I hadn't even heard the car arrive. I pushed myself up and off the settee, went to meet him in the kitchen and, with no time for greetings, launched in.

"What's going on?"

He shrugged as he shook his head. "No idea, b—"

I butted in before he got any further, "You must know something," and I regaled him with the details of the call I'd just received, talking quickly until he put his hands up to stop me mid-flow.

"If you let me finish, Em, I was sent to come and get you, but I have no idea what's going on. What I can tell you is that two helicopters have arrived. Cavendish in one, Trent in the other, each accompanied by a guy that I don't recognise, but both look like agents."

I pondered on this for a moment. "Why are Cavendish and Trent being kept apart? What would be the purpose of that? It could only be to prevent them from talking to each other, colluding perhaps? Don't you think? But what would they be colluding about? And why am I being summoned?" I realised I was just verbalising my thought process and knew Carlton couldn't help. He stared at me blankly as he shrugged no wiser than me and suggested we go.

There were far too many questions and keen to find the answers I picked up a thick jumper from the back of a chair I passed and pulled it over my head.

"Come on, then, you'd better take me to them."

Carlton grabbed the door handle to open it for me and I thrust my arms down into the sleeves of the jumper as I walked past him out of the cottage, calling back a goodbye to Susie.

We drove in silence to the Manor. Questions buzzed in my head, but I knew there was no point bombarding Carlton with them. He knew no more than I did.

He pulled into the courtyard. Although I could hear activity coming from the gym when we entered through the kitchens, they were eerily quiet considering it was only early evening. Carlton led the way towards Cavendish's large office and my nervousness increased the closer we got. I was feeling pretty much the same as I'd done the day I arrived for my interview, and if there had been room for them in my overcrowded insides I would have sworn butterflies had taken flight. I hated not knowing what I was about to face.

As we got closer, Carlton muttered, "All right?"

"As all right as can be expected," I replied, taking a deep breath which I let out slowly when we stopped at the door.

"You'll be fine," he reassured, clearly having no idea whether I would be or not, but then I was grateful to him when he pushed open the door and entered with me. I think he hoped he'd get to stay. I certainly wanted him to because I didn't know what I was up against. Trent's call had put me on edge, and I couldn't get rid of the feeling that somehow I'd done something wrong. It felt like being called in to see the headmaster. What if both Trent and Cavendish were against me for some reason? At least if Carlton stayed I'd have someone on my side.

I walked into the room, trying to project confidence, and stopped alongside Carlton to take in the scene, gleaning what I could. I was immediately drawn to Trent, who stood next to the fireplace and fixed me with his intense stare. He looked shockingly tired, pale and drawn with dark hollows under his eyes. I gave him a small, shaky smile that felt unsure on my lips and was not reciprocated by his. This was serious, I knew it, but with no clues I was bewildered as to why.

Nearest to Carlton and me was a man in a black suit, crisp white shirt, black tie, shoes polished to a high sheen; sharp jawline, sharper haircut, blond, blue-eyed, keen. He stared pointedly at Carlton. "You can go."

That made me dislike him immediately.

"I want him to stay," I retaliated, already knowing my request would be futile.

"No, he has to leave," was the response. It was not worth arguing the point. Carlton's hand moved into mine as he gave it a quick, comforting squeeze, and as I glanced over at him I was strengthened to see his reassuring smile. As quickly as that all happened, it was over. He'd turned and I heard the door closing behind me.

Trent moved towards me then. His expression hadn't changed, but as he got closer his eyes flashed a warning. As one arm started to go around me, he rested his other hand on my belly, checking in that all was well.

Blondie's hand intercepted him, holding him back.

"I am greeting my wife," Trent spat out disdainfully, shrugging the hand from his shoulder as his arms enclosed me in a hug. His cheek, two days of stubble, roughly brushed mine in a kiss as he whispered close to my ear, "We'll do all we can." At least I think that's what he said;

it was so quick and faint I couldn't be sure. I don't know if his words were meant to put me at my ease, but they only served to put me on my guard even further. What did he mean, they'd do all they could? This *was* something about me, but I didn't understand what. Nerves fluttered through my stomach once more in my uncertainty.

Blondie growled, "That's enough," and forcibly pushed us apart with his hands. I saw the anger flare in Trent's eyes, but he just raised his hands and stepped back, never taking his eyes from mine. Clearly now was not the moment to make a point with Blondie, but I sensed there was no love lost between them.

As Trent moved beside me his arm slid round and his hand rested on my hip. I felt ever so slightly buoyed by having him close to me. While I knew that this was something about me, whatever *it* was I now knew Trent and Cavendish were on my side – assuming that's who Trent had meant when he said 'we'. My attention was then taken by seeing Cavendish coming towards us, accompanied by someone else I didn't know. Black suit, white shirt, black tie, shoes – like a uniform. *Men in Black*. If only they'd been wearing sunglasses too, it would have made my day. This one was older, more worn – both him and his clothes – with none of the intensity of Blondie, who fairly fizzed with energy. I took to this one, dark hair, still short, brown-eyed, softer.

Big mistake.

Don't fall for that, I warned myself.

Good cop – bad cop.

Cavendish reached me and kissed my cheek lightly in greeting as if a meeting like this were an everyday occurrence. "You look well, Grayson." I smiled at him gratefully.

"Thanks, Cavendish, I am." I didn't reciprocate on the compliment; he appeared to be as exhausted as Trent, his tiredness deepening the lines that creased the corners of his eyes. I sounded nervous, which matched my emotional state, but I tamped down those feelings, not wanting to be so exposed as I looked at the two strangers.

Cavendish spoke smoothly, and sounded reassuring and confident as he introduced me.

"Grayson, I'd like you to meet Agents Bond and Rodwell." He indicated to Blondie first.

"No!" My face broke into a wide grin and I couldn't keep the incredulity out of my response, feeling Trent's hand tighten on my hip. "Agent Bond – really?" I looked round at the others, saw a glint in Cavendish's eyes, quickly suppressed as he cleared his throat, and a brief twitch of Trent's lips as I glanced at him which heartened me. Bond's face remained impassive. If anything his stare became even steelier. I didn't chance saying anything more – he'd probably heard it all before, but it did, if only for a brief moment, lighten my mood.

I reached out to shake hands with both the agents.

"Grayson, we've been talking with Bond and Rodwell here on and off for the last couple of days and they'd now like to talk to you." They'd talked to the agents for a couple of days? That was a lot of talking. Cavendish was understating it, so let's call it what it is, I thought: interrogation. I could sense a strain of sorts coming from both Trent and Cavendish, which could have been down to their tiredness.

"Okay, though I don't understand how any of your business has anything to do with me."

"I understand, Grayson, but let them ask their questions and then we'll see, shall we?" I nodded my agreement. Cavendish led me over to the settees and urged me to sit down and get comfortable. He offered me a choice of drinks, which I declined, wanting to get on and find out what this was all about.

Trent had relinquished his hold on me and taken up his place by the fire, right in my eyeline. He wasn't that far away, which I found comforting, and it was as though he was watching over me. I only had to glance up to be able to meet his eyes, and I knew he'd have planned it that way.

As Cavendish took up a place on the settee across the coffee table to me, but further down it towards the fireplace, Bond sat immediately opposite. He looked stiff and uncomfortable, and I thought he would probably have preferred to remain standing. Rodwell sat closer, on the settee at right angles to mine.

It was Bond who started.

"Grayson...I should be calling you Grayson, should I? I might be mistaken, but I thought you'd recently married Trent." He paused, then glanced over to make sure Trent fully appreciated the needling before he continued. "But you didn't take his name?" I remembered Trent telling me there were those in the security services who were unhappy with him being involved in Cavendish's enterprise, and the cheap dig where Bond could take it annoyed me. My reply was chilled.

"My name is Emma Trent, but for ease on the estate I'm still called Grayson. If you prefer to call me Mrs Trent instead, you are free to do so." I met his eyes as I responded and I did not blink. I didn't need to look at Trent to see his smile, it warmed me.

Bond looked as frosty as my retort.

"Okay, *Grayson*," he emphasised, "I'll get right to it. A package was received at headquarters a short while ago that was addressed to you." Silence followed, long and drawn out, and I fell at the first hurdle when being questioned. I felt the need to fill it.

"Are you expecting me to say something? That wasn't a question."

"What do you know about this package?"

"Nothing. Where is it?"

"That's none of your business."

"Yes it is. It was addressed to me, so surely it should've been delivered to me. You never know, I might then be able to tell you something about it." I was feeling cocky right at that moment and Bond ignored me.

"Let's go back to the beginning, shall we?" Silence fell again and I couldn't bear it, eventually giving in.

"The beginning of what?"

"Your life, Grayson. As far back as you can remember. Tell us about you and start with your maiden name."

I frowned at him a little dumbfounded, but he was serious. As four pairs of eyes watched me I told them what I knew, mystified as to the reason why. I felt a little foolish to begin with. What should I say? What should I leave out? As it turned out I didn't need to worry. As Rodwell watched and listened Bond directed the questioning, and piped up the moment he wanted any further details or clarification.

"My name was Emma Wills. I was orphaned when I was five years old and went to live with foster parents. My earliest memories are of them."

"What can you tell me of your parents?" he interrupted.

"Nothing. I don't remember my parents or anything before my first foster parents. I just said that."

He ignored my snappiness. "How long were you with your foster parents?"

"I only stayed with them for about two years, several different foster parents coming after. I moved every couple of years."

"Why?"

"I don't know. Perhaps I was a problem child." Irritation showed in my voice, but honestly, how was I meant to know why? I felt the need to maintain eye contact with him throughout this questioning; not wanting to appear as if I were seeking reassurance from Trent or Cavendish by checking in with them.

Bond didn't follow up with anything else, so I carried on. "I went to several different schools. Whichever one was local to my then current home. I started riding, and that was my main interest. I met Alex Grayson while in sixth form and we married at eighteen. I had an inheritance from my parents' estate which allowed us to buy a house."

I tried to gloss over Eva, but Bond insisted.

"We had a daughter, Eva, who died when she was six. Our marriage broke up."

"Because of Eva dying?" That was blunt.

"No, because my husband had an affair with Amy."

"Amy who?"

"Amy Grimes, my once best friend."

"Have you seen Alex recently?" At that point my eyes did flick across to Trent.

"Yes."

"Do you see him regularly?"

What has that got to do with anything?

"No."

"Are you in touch with Amy?"

"No."

"When was the last time you saw her?"

"The day I found her in bed with my husband." Not a flicker. The man had no empathy at all.

"How did you come to be working here?"

"I applied for the job."

"How?"

"How would you usually apply for a job? By replying to the advert, of course." I was starting to feel exasperated.

"Where did you see the advert?"

"It was put through my door, and before you ask, I don't know who by. At the time I assumed it was Amy."

"And now?"

"And now what?"

"Who do you *think* put it through your door now?"

"Still Amy, I guess."

"You guess?"

"Yes."

"Why?"

"Because of the lack of any other credible candidate who would have cared a damn about me."

And so it went on. Bond – always Bond – went over each point again and again as if to catch me out in a lie. Rodwell didn't say a word; he watched and listened. It was frustrating, an emotion I was not particularly good at hiding, but then Trent stepped in and, I could tell much to Bond's annoyance, halted proceedings.

"My wife is pregnant and needs a break." Although they must have clocked my condition, it hadn't been mentioned and I looked at him gratefully. On checking the time, I was surprised to find two hours had gone past. I needed a break, yes, but more than that I needed the toilet. Such is the lot of the pregnant woman. I was allowed to go, after my phone had been taken away from me. Cavendish showed me the way, and we were escorted by Bond, who stationed himself outside the door – which was off-putting.

When we returned to the office the tension in the air was palpable. It appeared that Trent and Rodwell had been having words, and we walked back in to Rodwell saying, "It's only because of Cavendish we came here to interview her at all. We would have preferred to have relocated to a place of our choosing." While I was grateful for Cavendish's influence, Trent didn't respond and I could feel his anger simmering as I sat back in the same seat. Positioned on the coffee table in front of me was a rectangular parcel, I guessed at about eight inches long, four inches wide and five inches tall, wrapped in brown paper. Tape had once sealed each end of the package, but now hung loose. I glanced over at Rodwell, who was again watching me, waiting, I felt, to see my reaction. I decided not to bite and ignored the package.

The questioning resumed, though actually it was just repeated. We went right back to the beginning again, topping up my frustration levels, and I couldn't help but feel that started to show in my responses.

Cavendish suddenly interrupted, "Look, is this level of questioning entirely necessary? I think Grayson has had enough. Could we not resume tomorrow?"

"No," Bond stated. "We need to get to a certain point tonight. However, if you have a problem with that we can arrange to have her taken elsewhere?" I imagined the 'elsewhere' he referred to wasn't going to be in a beautifully appointed room where I'd be interviewed on a comfortable settee. I was also sensing some hostility to me personally, which I didn't understand.

The questions started again. This time the focus was on my foster parents – names and addresses. I suddenly realised they were taking no notes, nor were they recording me, and it became clear what I was telling them wasn't anything they didn't already know. They were testing me, waiting for me to slip up, to give something away.

I told them what I could. There were blanks.

My first foster parents, when I was five, were Ben and Lisa Frampton who'd lived at 5 The Green, Thurlam.

When I was seven I went to David and Marjorie. I couldn't remember their surname. I couldn't remember where they lived.

When I was nine I went to Curtis and Fiona Mathers in a village called Norton, and I only remembered that because I remembered walking to Norton Primary School so we must have lived in the same place.

When I was twelve I went to Steve and Helen Morris, Drakes Close, Silton – I couldn't remember the number.

When I was thirteen I went to Marcus and Carol Smithers at The Rectory, Keston.

Finally, when I was fifteen I went to Brian and Sheila Skinner at 54 The Highway, Broadmead.

I thought I'd done pretty well.

"How come you remember the full names and address of the first pair, from when you were only five, but not of later ones?" Rodwell spoke, the first time he'd done so to me since we'd been introduced. There'd been no signal between them, but it was as if they had prearranged that at a certain point he would take over. His voice was softer, less accusatory than that of Bond.

I explained I'd gone back to try to see Ben and Lisa when I'd had Eva. I'd remembered they lived in Thurlam, and it wasn't too much of a stretch once I'd got there to find their cottage, situated as it was right in the centre, around the picturesque green.

"What did you find?" Rodwell again.

"That they'd moved away. I spoke to a next-door neighbour who had known them and told me their surname. She remembered me, and me leaving them."

"Did she tell you when they moved?"

"She told me they'd gone the night I left. That was why she'd remembered it, because she thought it was a bit odd." I could feel myself being drawn wide-eyed into an unavoidable trap. I didn't know why we were on this line of questioning or where this was heading, only that there was nothing I could do about it.

"And you didn't think that was strange?"

"At the time, yes…" I hesitated, "…but what was I meant to do about it?"

He tilted his head, nodding slightly. I thought I'd made a fair point, then he surprised me.

"David and Marjorie's surname was Brown and they lived at 48 High Street, Branham. Curtis and Fiona Mathers lived at 5 Blackthorn Drive. Steve and Helen

Morris lived at number ten." I thought he'd successfully filled in all the blanks, but couldn't be certain. The fact he'd done it without notes was impressive. I wondered why we'd been through the rigmarole of this line of questioning when they clearly knew the answers already.

"You've done your homework." My voice sounded a little croaky and I cleared my throat.

"Of course we have." He sat back and studied me a moment. "I don't know if you noticed, Grayson, but in each case I referred to the foster parents as *having* lived at that address. None of them still live at the address they lived at with you."

I frowned. "Not one?"

"Not one. Now what do you think the chances are of that?" He paused and I hoped this was a rhetorical question as I had no idea. I let the silence extend this time and left him to fill it. "And when do you think they moved out?" I had absolutely no idea – why would I have done? I shrugged as I shook my head, and he told me, his words slow and deliberate. "They all moved out the night you were taken from them to your next home, and we have, so far, been unable to trace any of them."

The silence after he'd spoken felt thick with anticipation. Questions raced through my mind, but not knowing which to ask first, I decided to keep quiet for the moment and see what else he divulged.

"As you have probably gathered by now, Grayson, we are thorough in our investigations. We check out every detail, follow up every lead, make sure every 'i' is dotted and 't' crossed, as it were, and the difficulty we have with you is this.

"Despite our extensive checks and cross-checks, we can find no record of you or any of your foster parents ever having been on the social service records. As far as we can tell, you have never been fostered with any registered foster family, nor have you ever been on the adoption register.

"In fact, Grayson, as far as the social services are concerned you have never existed."

Chapter 6

What? Completely confused, I looked over at Trent in bewilderment. He along with Cavendish looked as surprised as I did, and at that point Trent came over to sit next to me. He took my hand, which felt cold against his warm skin, and I appreciated the support.

"But that's ridiculous. I lived at each of those addresses with all of those people."

"We don't doubt that," Rodwell confirmed. "In some cases we've been able to track down and speak to neighbours and some have remembered you. But on whatever basis you were living with them then, it wasn't as part of the fostering system.

"Did you never think it odd that you were there as an only child? Most foster places are within families."

"No, I didn't," I ventured. "At least not at the beginning. How would I have known that it was anything other than normal? I'd been living like that since I was five, it was all I knew. It was only at my last school that I met someone else in foster care and realised how different my life was." I thought that was a good point. She lived in the town with a noisy family and had been with them for years. I remembered feeling a little envious of her settled situation.

Now it was as if I'd had the rug pulled from beneath my feet with regards to what I thought of my upbringing. I sat for a few moments, trying to get my head round this information, knowing it was going to take considerably longer than that to work through it. Pushing it to the back of my mind for the time being, I remained mystified as to why any of this would be the business of MI6.

"I appreciate everything you're saying, but I don't understand what interest it is of yours anyway where I lived, or with whom."

"It is of interest to us, Grayson, when it appears that you have infiltrated the security services. Albeit an external part of them, but nonetheless, you have come to our attention because our investigations reveal that you are not who you purport to be."

My anger erupted at that and I bit back at him sharply.

"This is not who I am *purporting* to be, this is who I have *believed* I am!"

Rodwell's eyes widened with surprise at my interjection.

I was angry. It felt as though they were making out I was up to no good here on the estate. What, did they think I was some sort of mole sent in to spy on the organisation? I wondered what Cavendish would think of that and looked over at him. He put his hand up to me, placating.

"It's all right, Grayson, we know you're not up to anything…" and he gave me a small smile which brought a twinkle to his eyes, "…of a nefarious nature here." With one word he took me straight back to my interview when I'd questioned him about the nature of the business on the estate. Trent squeezed my hand, and a thought suddenly came to me.

"But I had a background check done when I came here. Surely that would have revealed anything untoward…" I looked helplessly between Trent and Cavendish.

"It wasn't the same depth of check that has been carried out now," Trent replied. "We were mostly looking at your employment background and the basic personal stuff, nothing of this level." I wondered then how much he already knew of what was only now being revealed to me. Maybe over the last couple of days he and Cavendish had been briefed on me and my background as well as being questioned.

"But I have a birth certificate that confirms who I am." It sounded feeble, like I was trying to justify my existence. After everything that had gone before I wasn't surprised at the response I received.

"It's a fake," Bond confirmed.

My body sagged a little in defeat. I looked over at Bond and Rodwell. "So who am I?" I didn't know what else to say.

"Good question. Why don't you have a look at the package that arrived for you?" Rodwell indicated towards the parcel on the coffee table in front of me. I dropped Trent's hand and pushed myself forward on the settee so that I sat on the edge, then reached for the package and lifted it onto my lap.

"It's been opened."

"Of course it's been opened." Bond was back in the speaking role again. "If a package mysteriously arrives at headquarters it's taken away by security to be thoroughly investigated."

"You couldn't have just delivered it to me?"

"No…" He hesitated before elaborating. "It was sent as a message."

"How do you know?"

"Why else would it have been sent to us?" He had a point.

Something else occurred to me. "Why do you say 'mysteriously'?" For the first time, Bond appeared to be a little uncomfortable. He cleared his throat before replying.

"We're checking the security cameras to see if we can see who it was delivered by, but at the moment it seems as if one minute it wasn't there and the next it appeared on the desk."

My eyebrows rose slightly. "As if by magic?" I was teasing him a little; I could sense his discomfort at having to explain what appeared to be a breakdown in security. I didn't get a response other than his steely look intensifying and I let the moment pass.

"Can I open it?" He lifted his hand in a go ahead motion. I peered at the brown paper packaging. It was addressed, all capitals in thick black pen, to Mrs Emma Trent, care of the MI6 headquarters in London. I removed the paper to reveal a wooden box; it was dark golden brown, warm, the patina glossy, though worn round the edges. My fingers traced the inlaid pattern that ran around the top of the lid in a lighter wood as I tried to take in every detail. I was mystified as to why this would have been sent to me.

In silence, aware all eyes were on me, I opened the lid. The box was empty. I wasn't sure what I was expecting, but it wasn't for it to be empty. The lid was attached by brass hinges and there was a ridge of wood like a batten running around the inside, as if it'd once held something in place, such as a tray. I brought the box closer to my face to examine its interior, and it was at that moment I caught it: the faintest, faintest hint of a memory, so quick I almost missed it. I closed my eyes as I tried to focus; to repeat the experience. I needed more. There was nothing tangible so describing it as a memory was the only way I could explain it. Something from my past, and I couldn't even describe the scent. Warm wood? A spice? Smoke? A mingling of all of those? But it wasn't the scent itself that was important – it was the memory it evoked. Not even a memory though, not strong enough for that. A feeling, that's what it was, and that feeling was of something comforting and good…

In the periphery of my senses I was aware that Cavendish was speaking, saying the questioning had gone on for long enough. Rodwell and Bond were arguing they needed more before they could leave.

I put my hand into the box and pushed one end of the base down. A click, and the edges of a drawer showed as it popped from the base – less like a drawer, more like a hidden space.

Silence.

I glanced up to see all four men now sitting forward, staring intently at me.

"How did you know about that?" Rodwell asked, sounding puzzled. "I wasn't told that was there."

"Then it would appear your security department investigation was not that thorough after all, was it." I didn't even look at him as I spoke, nor did I bother to hide the dry sarcasm in my voice.

"You didn't answer my question."

"I don't know." And I really didn't, but something had been triggered by the 'memory' I'd smelt. However, my answer was distracted as I was more interested in the contents of the drawer that I'd taken by the edges and pulled further open. A stack of photographs were revealed, which I lifted out. By the look of the haphazard pile that now sat on my hand they were not a set, but more like individual photos taken from a variety of cameras over the ages.

The first, fading with a slight yellowish sheen to all its colours, was of a young woman, pretty and pale with dark hair – big hair, long, dark curls – sitting on a settee. A baby was wrapped tightly in a blanket in her arms. From her expression, it was clear her focus had been on the baby someone having called to her to look up. Reluctantly made to drag her attention away from the bundle in her arms, she had fleetingly met the camera with a look filled with a mixture of delight, pride and happiness. I imagined the moment the shutter had closed, her eyes turning back towards the baby. I remembered that same intensity of feeling when I'd had Eva.

I passed the photo on to Trent.

The second showed a toddler wearing dungarees and a T-shirt with bare chubby feet, just walking, perhaps only just standing, taken up close. Its hands were above its head, fingers tightly gripping those of an adult for support as it struggled gamely to take the next step. Blue eyes, flushed cheeks, its mouth was open showing a few pearly white teeth.

The third was, I assumed, the same child, older – three or four – painting at a table, concentrating intently on the job in hand, the tip of her tongue visible at the corner of her mouth. A girl, and there was something familiar about her. Her hair was longer and pulled back into a loose ponytail, from which most of it seemed intent on escaping, wisps falling across her face. Her mother sat next to her – or I assumed it was her mother. It was the same woman, anyway, from the first photo. My eyes flicked back to the girl.

Something familiar about her?

She looked like Eva, but she wasn't.

Eva had looked like me…

Her mother next to her.

My heart lurched as I gasped. *My mother next to me?* My throat tightened and tears welled as I looked at the mother's face, frantically trying to find something I could honestly say I recognised, but there was nothing. And if it was my mother, how sad was that?

I didn't utter a word as I passed each photo along to Trent for him to look at, then he handed them along to Cavendish, and so on round the circle. I left them to draw their own conclusions.

The rest of the photos told the story of me growing up through all those awkward, gawky years, becoming more and more recognisable as me as the photos progressed. Through the school years, a variety of school uniforms were on show depending on which school I was attending at that moment in time.

Then, pretty soon in the pile came the first photos of me riding. I recognised the ponies, and later on the horses.

A photo of Alex and me, our sixth form selves, his arm slung across my shoulders on our walk home from school. Another of us as we left our house in Crowthorpe.

Then more of Eva, firstly being carried in a car seat, then as a little girl as Alex and I swung her between us as we walked down the road, our delight clear as she squealed with laughter. Another memory brought back to me.

Me alone, sitting on a bench, taken from the other side of the churchyard.

The last one was of Trent and me kissing in the gardens of the Manor, him in a charcoal-grey suit, my dress elegant, the train like cream pooling on the grass behind me.

The photos all had three things in common: they were taken outside; they were taken at a distance; they were taken without my knowledge.

I waited as the photos did the rounds then collected them all back into the pile which I kept close to me. No one spoke, and I wasn't about to discuss what appeared self-explanatory. I looked over at Rodwell.

"You didn't know about these photos, so I'm not sure how you jumped to the conclusion that this empty box was a message being sent to you."

He tilted his head in acknowledgement and reached into his inside jacket pocket.

"It seems to me these photos," and he indicated to the pile in my hand, "are a message for you, not us. The box wasn't empty when it arrived. I took this out. I didn't want you to get distracted."

And he handed me another photo, taken this summer. Two men: Trent and Cavendish; two women: Grace and me, standing on the steps of the courthouse. I remembered it well – we'd just come out of the inquest into Zoe's death. Three crosses, drawn roughly at the places our hearts would be, marked Trent, Cavendish and me.

A circle enclosed the cross over my heart.

I felt Trent stir next to me then move closer as he caught sight of the photo. He took it gently from me as his hand ran up my back, caressing and soothing me. I watched him, his features darkening as he peered closer at the photo, flipping it over to check out a mark on the back that I hadn't seen. He then passed it wordlessly on to Cavendish.

"It's okay," he muttered, "we'll sort this out." I didn't know what he meant by that, but I did know we had now all caught up on the who-knew-what-when part of the questioning. Judging by their reactions, neither Trent nor Cavendish had seen this photo before.

"I don't know what this means," I said to no one in particular. I'd have been happy for anyone to explain. I was watching Cavendish as he studied the photo.

"Grayson?" Rodwell drew my attention to him and I noticed he took a deep breath, letting it out before continuing. "This photo is the message. It is most unusual, but we are being tipped off that a hit has been taken out on the three of you. You see the mark on the back?" I shook my head absently as I was still focusing on his words – 'a hit' – assuming they meant what I thought they meant. The photo had done the rounds and he handed it back to me. When I turned it over I saw a small circle with a V and a Z written over each other inside it. I shrugged. It meant nothing to me, and I handed the photo back to Rodwell.

He studied me for a moment, then asked, "Does the name Zakhar Volkov mean anything to you?"

"No." I felt bewildered by the direction this conversation was going in.

"He is a person of significant interest to the security services, although we have little intelligence on him. We don't know where he is, or what he looks like. Unfortunately, however, we do know what he does. This is his mark on the back of the photo. He has been in touch with us since this was received and told us that it was him who delivered the package." He paused, as if to take a moment to assess what he was about to say. I didn't take my eyes from him; my breathing was shallow and by consequence I was a little light-headed, but I willed him to continue. I needed to hear it all.

"He is an assassin, Grayson, and the photo was given to him by his clients as his next hit. The circle around the cross on your chest depicts you as the primary target."

The information was coming hard and fast and I felt the blood draining from my head. This was way too much, and I had the horrible feeling there was more to come. My chest was tight and I seemed unable to take a deep breath. I held on to Trent's hand tightly, feeling my skin becoming clammy and cold with fear. I tried to think clearly. Why was I being targeted? I didn't need to think long on this: it could only be Orlov. I'd made a fool of him and this was his vengeance. Not man enough to come back to do the job himself, I noted, instead he'd sent someone else to do his dirty work.

Though hang on a minute. My eyes narrowed in thought and I turned to Rodwell. It was as if he was waiting for me to process the information and come to my own conclusion.

"Why is he telling you this? Why is he tipping you off?"

"A very good point, Grayson. Why indeed? And this is where the mystery about you deepens. Volkov sent the photo to us to get our attention and deliver a warning. He has told us he sent the box as a message for you. And although you told us you didn't know how you knew about the secret compartment, clearly the box awakened some sort of memory for you, enabling you to find it and the photos. I think we can all see the story in the photos and it backs up what Volkov has told us."

"Which is what?" I asked, irritated with his hesitation, wanting him to spit it out and at the same time not wanting to hear what was coming next.

Rodwell looked seriously at me as though about to impart bad news, then watched me closely as he delivered the punchline.

"Volkov has told us he is your father."

Chapter 7

I didn't sleep a wink I was so unsettled, the events of the evening whirling in my mind. Trent and I had sat up talking for a couple of hours when we got back, by which time he'd gone grey with exhaustion, and was now asleep next to me having been seriously deprived over the last couple of days.

Baby wriggled and squirmed in my stomach as if depicting the turmoil in my mind. When Rodwell had broken the news it was as if the air had been sucked from the room and I'd sat there, stunned. Completely stunned. Silence had fallen around me as all watched for my reaction, which when it came had been lame.

"How can he be? My parents are dead." It was stating the obvious, but I had no idea how I should have reacted to this news.

Rodwell had answered, "I know that's what you've grown up thinking, Grayson, but he has given us information on you that I have been able to verify. Shocking though it may be, I believe him." I'd scoffed at that point, not wanting to accept it, and Rodwell had patiently continued, "Information, I might add, that we've been able to substantiate through our investigations and our questioning of you, Trent and Cavendish. I needed to see how that questioning went, which is why we have given you a hard time this evening, and I have to say it has strengthened his position. Honestly, Grayson, I believe him," he added, for the second time and unnecessarily in my opinion. It was as if Rodwell was on Volkov's side and was trying to vouch for him.

"But how…" I'd wanted to ask how my father could be alive; how he could be an assassin; how he could have been given the contract to kill me and Trent and Cavendish. I'd wanted to ask so much, but didn't know where to start, or what they'd actually be able to answer, so I'd plumped for, "So why haven't I been with him? Why did I grow up with foster parents?" Then I'd remembered the other revelation of the evening. "Who weren't actually foster parents at all, it turns out."

"He told us he organised for you to be unofficially fostered. It was one of the pieces of information we could check out on you," Rodwell confirmed.

"But how do you go about doing that? And why? Why not just hand me over to social services?"

Rodwell had shaken his head regretfully. "I'm sorry, Grayson, I don't have much more I can help you with." He'd paused, then landed me with another verbal right hook. "Though he would like to meet you. Perhaps you could ask him then."

I'd sat up straighter, bristling.

"Would he? He hasn't wanted to know me up to now, but suddenly he wants to meet me?" My voice had risen a little and Trent had started on the soothing motion with his hand on my back again. I'd given it a few moments' thought then. There was so much I needed to know and it would be better going straight to the source for the information, no doubt about that.

"Make the arrangements," I'd told them. I'd sounded strong, but by that point I was anything but. My head reeled from the overload of information it had received over the course of the evening.

Bond had been remarkably quiet during the latter part of the discussions, and his attitude had softened towards me now it appeared I clearly had no idea of my connection to Volkov and apparently wasn't a spy in their midst. Sounding more sympathetic he'd said, "We'll get a DNA test done at the same time if you're agreeable. It would be a sensible thing to do." I'd mumbled my agreement to this and watched them get up to leave. They'd said their goodbyes to Cavendish, but ignored Trent, who hadn't seemed to mind, although I had. A tiny flare of anger hissed among the confusion that reigned in my brain, then they'd left the room.

Cavendish had told me to go home, get some rest and not to worry. Not to worry! Trent had then guided me home and we'd exhausted ourselves – or rather, I'd exhausted him by making him go over his last few days, trying to glean any bit of additional information I could. He'd filled me in on his experiences, which didn't amount to much more than I'd already been able to work out for myself. He and Cavendish had been separated as soon as they'd arrived at headquarters and both had been questioned on and off over the last couple of days along the same sort of lines as this evening. He hadn't had the opportunity to talk to Cavendish at all, but they would debrief in the morning and see what should be done from there.

Trent had insisted I go to bed, but while I lay there awake, knowing I'd suffer the next day, I was completely unable to switch off. So many questions were left unanswered. Although Trent had warned me against immediately believing Volkov was my father, stating that he could be some sort of fraudster, I couldn't see why anyone in his position would pretend to be something he wasn't. What would be in it for him? Trent had to admit I was probably right, but still wanted me to be cautious and not get my hopes up.

But I didn't know if my hopes were actually up.

I felt a bit peculiar about it in all honesty and I was confused about how I was meant to feel. Thrilled that my supposedly dead father had made contact? Frightened, or horrified, by his chosen career? Angry that he had left me alone all these years? Sad at the wasted opportunity to be part of a proper family? And then, right at the heart of it, something I'd never thought of, never believed could be a possibility. If my father was alive, then could the same be said of my mother?

I got up the next morning before the alarm. Leaving Trent to sleep on, I went to let Susie out. I watched her sniff round the garden, catching up with the smells of creatures that had passed through during the night. I leaned against the doorframe, cold damp air settling on my skin as I gazed out at what was so far a grey drizzly day.

After feeding Susie I made toast and tea which I sat and ate at the kitchen table, staring at the wooden box that sat in the middle. I hadn't opened it since the first time, unable to look at the photos again yet. Rodwell had tried to take it with him the previous evening. It was 'evidence' apparently, but I'd hung on to it and told them no. He didn't press the issue.

I thought I'd have a look at them again later...maybe.

I showered and dressed, managing not to wake Trent, and went over to the yard to start work. I always fed the horses first, today only half listening to their gathering impatience as I mixed their feed. Monty spun circles in his stable over and over, churning the straw until it resembled a whirlpool then dashing back to the door to see if I was coming yet. Benjy kicked at the lower partition of his door with his front foot in his annoyance at having to wait. I delivered the bowls and left them to it while I fussed Susie for a few minutes, which would be all it took for them to clear their hard food away.

I changed the ponies' night rugs for waterproof ones and led them out to the field. It had been a wet spring and there'd been a lot of rain over the last couple of days so my feet squelched into the saturated ground as we approached the field. If it got any worse I'd have to arrange to have some wood chips delivered to prevent the ground getting any more poached, I thought morosely as I reached the gate. The ponies, as if picking up on my subdued mood, wandered off quietly to start grazing. I watched them for a moment before walking back to the stables.

I made up a couple of hay nets and fixed one to the fence before tying the other up in Regan's box for him to start on, then I led Monty out and tied him up. Giving him a quick brush down, I got the straw out of his mane and tail and adjusted his rugs. The horses weren't going to be exercised today, but I thought if it cleared up a bit later I'd turn them out for an hour or two. They weren't going to be clipped out again, so as their coats grew back in I could harden them off through the spring by turning them out more often.

I mucked out Monty's box, needing the physical work as I cleared my mind of everything but the job in hand. Being around the horses was great therapy for me, it always had been, and having Susie hanging around the stables as I worked through my jobs helped as well. Finishing Monty's stable, I filled his water buckets and returned him and his hay net to it before going through the same routine with Regan.

I was putting him back in his box as Trent joined me. He leaned on the post-and-rail fence.

"You should have woken me."

"You needed to sleep."

"You look like you could use some too." I'd already clocked the dark rings under my eyes earlier and didn't need reminding. I shrugged.

"You didn't need to do this this morning, Em, you could have got Turner in."

"I did need to do it. I needed to work to keep my mind occupied." The fact I'd just gone through the motions on autopilot didn't come into it.

"Do you want to talk?"

"No," I shook my head, adding, "thanks," as an afterthought. What was there to say?

He hesitated for a moment. "Cavendish and Grace are coming over." I looked down, nodding. "Carlton and Greene as well..."

"Oh...they know?"

"They've been briefed."

I started sweeping down the yard. "I'll finish this and I'll be in."

I was crossing back to the cottage when the others arrived. By the time I'd got my boots off and washed my hands they'd all followed me in. Greene gave me a big supportive hug as she passed me, though she didn't say a word. Trent was in the process of making mugs of coffee for everyone and, after subdued greetings, we sat round the table. No one appeared to have slept well. The wooden box sat in the middle and as everyone got themselves settled the silence stretched out into awkwardness.

Grace reached out a hand and covered mine. "How are you, Emma?" Tears stung my eyes that were raw with lack of sleep.

"Fine..." my voice cracked as I smiled gratefully at her, "...but don't be nice to me, Grace, I can't take that at the moment." She squeezed then patted my hand before moving hers away.

"So," Cavendish started briskly, "we need to come up with a plan on how to proceed." He looked round the table. "My suggestion is that we aim to set up a meeting with Volkov as soon as possible. Within the week. The samples for the DNA test will be done there, although I suspect that is a mere formality..." and he glanced over at me worriedly as he cleared his throat. "Grayson, are you still all right to meet him? We could just do the tests and wait for the results if you prefer."

"No, I'll meet him. I doubt he would have the proof he has or have gone to the lengths he has done if he wasn't my father."

"True. Are you happy to meet him at the Manor rather than here? I think it's probably best if we keep it semi-formal."

Trent was nodding as I agreed.

"Okay then. I'm going to call a meeting of all the staff this evening to brief everyone on the current position." I hadn't thought of that, but it was sensible, everyone getting the same message.

Carlton interrupted, "Just going back to setting up the meeting with Volkov, I think there should be several of us present until we know exactly who he is and what he wants."

"I agree," came from Trent.

Cavendish responded, "I think if we are all there that will be enough, and we'll have some additional security outside the room."

"We need to go over the security on the estate again anyway. It's become lax. We'll cover that tonight."

"Can I ask how this is being arranged with Volkov? If anyone knows, that is…" Greene glanced round at each of us as she spoke, her eyes coming back to Cavendish.

"We don't know yet, but what do you mean exactly?"

"He must have done things that he could be charged for…Sorry, Emma." She glanced across at me, but I shook her look away. It wasn't as if I hadn't already thought the same thing a million times during the night. She continued, "So I'm wondering on what basis has he come forward, and depending on that how is he coming here? As a prisoner? As someone S.I.S. are working with?"

"We don't know yet," Trent responded. "I suspect he's aiming to do a deal to gain his freedom from prosecution in exchange for helping with information, be that in general or specifically to get us closer to the organisation.

He won't come in via the agency unless they are able to offer him some form of protection. He has no need to – he could turn up whenever he likes."

"What do you mean by that?" Grace sounded alarmed.

Trent looked over at me. "Emma, do you mind?" and he gesticulated towards the box. I shook my head and reached out to pull it towards me, then opened the lid. Once I'd collected the photos together again the previous evening I'd put them back in the hidden drawer, so I popped that open to retrieve them, much to the interest of those who hadn't seen it before. Pausing to look at the top one for a moment...*my mother*...I then handed them round the table – the story of me growing up. Not much was said apart from a cheeky comment from Carlton on the relative gawkiness of me as a young teen which earned him a glare, though I had to smile. He was quite right.

The photos did the rounds, finishing with the one of Trent and me kissing in the Manor gardens at our wedding.

Trent then answered Grace's question. "Apart from the first few photos, all of these have been taken at a distance and, more importantly, without Emma knowing about it. The last one shows he was on the estate, and we weren't aware of it. Volkov goes by his reputation – no one even knows what he looks like – so I suggest we let him come to us whichever way he thinks is best."

The rest of the week passed excruciatingly slowly, but eventually we had word that Volkov would be with us early evening on the Saturday. The agency had said they wanted to have a couple of agents present, and when Cavendish coolly informed them a couple of agents were already going to be present they were apparently a bit sniffy. However, they couldn't do much about it.

I asked Turner to do evening stables for me so I could be up at the Manor early and got the distinct impression he would rather have come with me. Since the meeting of all the staff he'd been around the stables every moment he could and Trent had taken to calling him my shadow again. Amid all my other worries, it crossed my mind that perhaps we should be more concerned for his mental health, but he appeared quite happy and settled. When I chatted to him one day he said he was just enjoying working with the horses. Who was I to deny him that?

I was back in Cavendish's office again and pacing the floor as we waited. Trent urged me to sit down, saying I'd wear myself out, but I couldn't. I'd been like this all week: restless. It was now April and only a few weeks until the birth, and I realised I should have been taking it easy, but whenever I went to sit another anxiety would grab me and I'd be on the move again. I was concerned what all the stress would be doing to the baby as well, but at least with me moving around a lot, it slept. I rationalised that in its sleeping state it wouldn't feel the stressful vibe coming from me.

The last time we'd been together in the office had been on the previous Monday evening when all the staff were there. Cavendish and Trent had passed on the intelligence relating to my family background, which I found incredibly awkward to sit through, my cheeks pink with embarrassment. There were audible gasps as they revealed who my father was and I felt terrible thinking all these people could be putting themselves in jeopardy again, and because of me this time.

Trent tried to reassure me that, until they took care of the top men, it was only ever going to be a matter of time before the Polzin organisation struck back. He told me to remember that three people had been on the contract given to Volkov, and me being one of them showed Orlov's involvement and his rank within the organisation. It also showed his weakness: he wanted vengeance against me purely because I'd made him look a fool. Trent made the point that if Volkov hadn't been my father the hit could have been taken by now and we'd already be dead. At least this way we had some time.

The office was now quiet. Grace sat near the fireplace and gazed into space. I could only imagine at her worries with all that was happening and the children being due home for the holidays soon. Cavendish was at his desk at the far end of the room, dealing with some correspondence Sharpe had left for him. Trent, Carlton and Greene stood together by the office door chatting, but their voices were soft, only reaching me as a mumble.

I paced from one side of the room to the other in front of the four floor-to-ceiling windows behind Cavendish's desk that looked out onto the garden. Forster was on duty, ready for any arrivals via the main gate. Porter was ready at the farm; every entrance approachable, but monitored. I got to the wall, turned and started my walk back, passed by one window, past the second, on to the third.

I stopped.

Something made me.

A feeling.

An intuition.

And I turned to the window and looked directly into the face of a man I could have sworn I'd never seen in my life before.

I stood, staring, and he stared right back, holding that connection less than six feet the other side of the glass. I couldn't read his expression, but I saw it soften, his eyes crinkling slightly at the corners as the briefest hint of a smile touched his lips. Before this day, in the build-up to it, I'd tried to come up with an image of him, but had drawn a blank. I'd decided that when I saw him I'd recognise him, but now here we were, face to face, and all I felt was confusion as to why I didn't. I spent a moment, taking him in: dark hair, greying at the sides, thick and curling, though shorter than Trent's; lean build; taller than me; dressed in black, from the boots right up to the trench coat that hung open.

"He's here," I heard Trent behind me, then he and Cavendish reached my side. I stepped back as Trent unlocked the window, swinging it open like a door to let our guest in. Volkov entered, his eyes still on me, and stood silently as the window was locked behind him.

Trent led me a little further away as Carlton approached Volkov, who removed his coat then spread his arms out to the sides, allowing Carlton to pat him down. When Carlton was satisfied he stepped back and Cavendish held out his hand to shake Volkov's. Then he introduced everyone in the room, as a formality rather than anything else. I had no doubt Volkov knew exactly who everyone was.

Cavendish left me to last.

"And, of course, this is Emma." Everyone else had shaken hands with Volkov so I followed suit, not sure what he expected from me.

"Emma," both of his hands enclosing mine, "it's a pleasure after so long..." His voice was like a rumble, deep and softly accented. I didn't know what to say, but my face must have given me away. He stalled for a moment, then carried on and I registered disappointment in his voice: "You don't recognise me, do you?" I shook my head. "No, no, of course not..." he muttered, more to himself than to any of us. "That's as it should be."

I wasn't sure what he meant by that.

Feeling awkward I didn't know what to do next, but Cavendish stepped in and suggested we all sit down and sort out a few of the formalities. I was grateful. Out of all the ways I'd thought this meeting was going to go, me suddenly becoming mute and not having a thing to say for myself was not among them.

Grace organised some drinks while we got ourselves settled and Cavendish called for Bray to come to the office. I knew she was going to be taking the samples for DNA testing. I sat on the settee with Trent. Volkov sat opposite alongside Greene. Carlton remained standing by the fireplace.

"How are you, Emma...and your baby?" Casting a glance at my stomach, he added, "Not many weeks now?"

"Er...no, four or five, and we're fine, thanks...both of us."

He nodded and gave the briefest of smiles as he said, "That's good." His eyes flickered away and I was suddenly aware it wasn't only me that was nervous. A moment later Bray entered the room along with West carrying the tray of drinks. The next few minutes were taken up with Bray handing Volkov and me swabs which we ran round the inside of our cheeks before handing them back. She placed them separately in long tubes, screwing them tightly closed. After giving me a big smile, she left.

Trent poured me a glass of water and I took a sip, as much to be doing something as anything. I watched as Grace handed out the drinks. Volkov thanked her politely as she handed him a glass, giving her a half smile from a face that didn't look like it smiled much. He was what I guess you would describe as craggily handsome; clean shaven, the lines on his face were deep and my impression was they appeared to have been etched by worry and sadness rather than laughter.

As we settled again, Trent took the lead. "I think it's probably best if we have a brief chat about the overall situation, and then if it's okay with the two of you," and he gesticulated between Volkov and me, "we'll give you some time to talk." He raised his eyebrows in question and we both agreed.

"Okay. So, Volkov, perhaps you can fill us in on your relationship with the Polzin organisation."

"Of course," and he sat forward a little, leaning his elbows on his knees. "The work I do is on a client by client, contract by contract basis. I haven't solely worked for the Polzins, but they were the ones who were first interested in my abilities and I have done several jobs for them over the years."

"How many years?"

"Thirty."

"I know you are aware that we are working towards closing their organisation down but we want to know if you are willing to help us."

"I am aware. I have seen what is happening from outside and inside and I will do everything I can to help."

"We are having difficulty getting to the heads of the family."

"I understand, though I suspect the situation is not as you think it to be."

"How so?" interrupted Cavendish. Volkov turned to him as he answered.

"It is thought there are two older brothers in overall charge, but that has changed. One died last year, dropped dead of a heart attack, and the other is terminally ill with cancer. Anatoly has all but taken over. I have known him since he was ten, much younger than his brothers. A surprise, if you like, for his parents, or sadly more like a mistake, and a nasty one at that. I have never met a more brutal man.

"Orlov is still his right-hand man, his second in command – whatever you want to call it. Between them they lead the rest."

"So there aren't children of the older brothers already grown up and ready to take up the reins then?"

"There have been children, but several girls," he shrugged as if it were unlikely a girl would be considered a suitable heir for such a business, "and a couple of boys, but none have shown an interest or been deemed to be of the right calibre to take over. So it's in Anatoly's hands. He does have two boys, currently teenagers and possibilities for the future. They are sadistic little shits – pardon me – and fortunately too young at present. If you could close this down now it would bring an end to the business once and for all."

"Do you know where Anatoly and Orlov are?"

"I could tell you where they were the last time I saw them, but that would do you no good as they will have moved on. They move regularly and security around them is tight – tighter than you can possibly imagine. Many is the time I have thought of killing them. That is my job, after all, but I would never stand a chance. They know who I am and what I am capable of and they take precautions. I am searched before I can see them and am never left alone with any of them."

"You've thought about killing them yourself?" Trent questioned, interested and clearly wanting more information and Volkov gave a grunt in agreement, then clarified.

"I'm a sniper by speciality and have considered organising my own hit on them, but over the years there have always been too many people around them. You can't kill that many in one go, and they would only have to find my bullets in a body to mean an end for me," he glanced over at me, "and I had someone I needed...no, wanted to stay alive for."

"That brings me on to another point, Volkov," Cavendish said. "Last year...it was you on the estate, wasn't it? You who took out the man at the stables?"

"Yes, that was me." He looked at Grace, then over at me. "You did very well, I was so proud of you." I could feel my cheeks growing warm as I blushed in that irritating way I did whenever I was complimented.

"Thank you." My voice was thick as I cleared my throat.

"So why did you just do that, on that evening, if you were with the Polzins?" Trent asked, sounding puzzled.

"Oh, they didn't know I was there. I was not *with* them. But I knew they were coming to attack you and thought I'd be here to step in if I was needed. I was able to help in a minor way...you did all the rest." Brushing off the part he'd played, he included Grace as he raised his hands to indicate to whom he referred. "I can tell you, I have never seen Orlov so angry – and all because his ego had been bruised, of course."

"Why has it taken so long for them to retaliate?" Trent queried.

"You have been keeping them busy over the winter, constantly breaking down and damaging various parts of their network. They are on their own now in the leadership role, don't forget, and it has taken a while to pull things together. Eventually though enough was enough, but rather than deal with it themselves they contracted me to do it."

"And Emma is the primary target?" Trent asked. Volkov stared at him for a moment before answering.

"Yes, the instruction I have is to kill her first. Orlov's idea in order to cause *you*," and he stared pointedly at Trent, "maximum pain. It shows the influence he has over Anatoly to get him to agree."

"How long do we have?" Trent's voice was low.

"They will expect me to have completed the contract by the middle of April. I'm given time, and with three on the list extra time, but by then they will want results."

The room went quiet, everyone deep in thought. Then Cavendish spoke. "Can I suggest you stay here, Volkov? Defect, if you want to give it a name."

"Thank you for the offer, but I can't. If I don't go back, if they can't check in with me when they expect to be able to, they will be suspicious and start investigating. It won't take long and they will come and we need to give Emma as much time as possible, ideally for her to have the baby."

I knew that was never going to happen. Baby wasn't due until the beginning of May; the Polzins were never going to be fobbed off until then.

"Can I ask why you still do work for them? Why don't you just walk away?"

Volkov looked away from Cavendish and down into his lap, taking a deep breath.

"I have tried to leave. I hate what I do…" His voice tailed off and he appeared downcast. "But they know I have a daughter that I have hidden from them. Over the years they have made many attempts to find you…" he met my eyes, "…every time I stepped out of line. Every time I've tried to leave, there has been that threat hanging over me, and I know they will see it through. I have seen what they will do. They have told me what they would do to her when they find her. This is the closest they have ever been, and yet, at the moment, they still have no idea who Emma is.

"I will do whatever it takes to protect her, but time is running out and my hand has been forced by being given this contract. I need to work with you to try and bring them down before they find out who she is and come for her."

Goosebumps prickled my skin as a chill ran down my spine and Trent tensed beside me as Cavendish spoke up.

"Thanks, Volkov, you've been open with us which we appreciate and I'll tell you where we stand. Emma is part of our family here, and as I have told her we are forever in her debt after her actions in saving my family last year. We, and I mean the whole of the estate when I say that, are united in protecting her. I promise you we will do all we can in helping you bring them down."

I was grateful to Cavendish for his support, then something clicked into place when Volkov spoke again.

"I was delighted when you took her on here, Cavendish. I'd heard about what you were doing and wanted her to be part of—"

"It was you," I interjected.

"What was?" Volkov was suddenly wary.

"It was you who put the advert through my door." He tilted his head in acknowledgement of the truth. "Why?"

"Like I said, I wanted you here and you needed a new start. I thought it would be safe for you to be under the protection of these people, though I had no idea then of the work they would be taking on. I thought you would enjoy being with the horses. I know they've helped you before."

I hated the thought that he'd had any part to play in me being employed here; that I hadn't got the job on my own merit.

"I wasn't the only applicant – you couldn't be sure I would get the job."

"Your competition wasn't that difficult to get rid of."

I stared at him aghast as I remembered the ex-Household Cavalry man Trent had told me about.

"Oh my God, what did you do to him?"

Volkov took in my shocked face and realised what he'd said, reaching out his hand as if to pacify me.

"Oh, no, no, no, Emma, I didn't do what you're thinking. I am not an animal. I paid him off to withdraw his application, that was all."

Well that was okay, then. That was just fine. Daddy paid out to get me into a job. His interference caused anger to prickle through me.

There had been enough talk for now, at least between all of us. Volkov, Trent and I were left alone. Although Grace was the only one who left, the others dissipated to other parts of the office. Cavendish returned to his desk, and Carlton and Greene moved to the far side of the room where they sat chatting quietly. No one apparently trusted Volkov enough to leave me alone with him yet.

Trent looked at me, his thumb running across the knuckles of the hand he held. "Are you okay with this?" I felt stronger after my ice-breaker exchange with Volkov so after confirming I was indeed okay with this he gave my hand a quick squeeze, let it go and went over to join Cavendish at his desk. I watched him move the chair to make sure he could keep us in view at the same time as talking to Cavendish.

Volkov moved closer, onto the settee set at right angles to the one I was on. He glanced over at Trent, indicating towards him as he muttered, "He seems like a good man."

"He is."

"I hadn't anticipated *that* happening when you came here."

"Well perhaps you're not able to influence everything after all." I knew I sounded as spiky as I felt. I may have mellowed over many things since coming to the estate, but I still didn't like being controlled.

"Emma, I'm sorry. I was only doing what I thought best for you..." He tailed off and I started to relent – a little.

"Okay, let's move on shall we?" Though I wondered where we went from here.

"I can only imagine how this discovery has been for you, Emma. I have been living with the truth of our situation forever, and you are only just embarking on that path. Please, ask me anything you like. I promise to be honest with you."

"I don't know where to start," and that was the truth of it; my hand rested on my stomach as Baby moved inside. I imagined him waking from his nap, yawning, trying to stretch tiny fists up above his head. There was precious little room for that now. My stomach was taut and I wondered how it was going to be possible for me to get any bigger.

I decided to steer clear of the personal. Stick with business and see where it led. "You said you didn't only work for the Polzins. If you despise what you do so much, even if you had no choice other than to work for them, why do you still also work for others?"

"The honest answer is that I do it for the money. I'm not proud of what I do, Emma, but I am good at it and others seek out my services. I don't seek to justify my actions to you and I know exactly where I shall be going when I leave this life, but outside of the Polzin work I live by my own rules. A code, if you like. I kill only those who have inflicted the worst atrocities on others and have gone unpunished through the traditional routes. Rapists, paedophiles, murderers mostly – and believe me, I'm not unaware of the irony of the last one.

"I get given a contract, I carry out my research on the target until I'm satisfied they are guilty of what they are being accused of, then I take the appropriate action." This revelation caused a confused reaction in me. Was he a good guy? A bad guy? I didn't know. The line was so blurred I doubted I ever would know. I guessed it all came down to your perception of right and wrong.

"So you're a vigilante for hire?"

"Yes, I guess I am, though they are so often depicted as the hero and that is not how I see myself."

"Where are you from?" His English was perfect, but the accent was there.

"Russia. A small village originally, but I've never been back." I was at least half Russian then. As I thought this I realised that, DNA test notwithstanding, I'd already accepted Volkov was my father.

"Why did you get involved with the Polzins in the first place?"

He sighed. "They spotted my potential early on, encouraged me, complimented me. I was young and I was trying to support your mother and raise a family. No…" He hesitated, shaking his head. "No, that's not right. I promised you the truth, Emma, and the truth is I was foolish. All the attention went to my head and I thought

102

too much of myself. I was blinded by the money and was in way too deep before I realised what they wanted of me. Once I'd killed one person they had that over me and I was still only twenty. It took another three years before I had the guts to tell them I wasn't going to work for them again. I left…"

My mother? He'd mentioned her and I couldn't help focusing on that. There was more coming, I knew it, feeling a chill run through me, a warning, a fear of finding out. I reluctantly prompted him.

"What happened?"

He focused on his hands for a moment. Then he looked up at me and gave it to me straight.

"They took their revenge. They chased your mother one night when she was driving to visit a friend. Chased her in their cars until she drove hers off a bridge. She was later than I expected coming back and as soon as I heard of the crash on the news, I knew." Flooded with disappointment, I felt the pinprick of tears. However unlikely it had been that she was still alive, I'd been banking on that far more than I'd realised and my spirits sank.

"Oh…"

"I'm sorry, Emma." His voice was gentle and I looked up to meet his gaze.

"Did you love her?"

"More than you can imagine. She was everything to me."

"Do you have someone else in your life now? Someone special?"

"No. There have been other women, I won't lie, but no one special."

I thought for a moment. Something in what he'd said was nagging at me.

"I don't understand. Once she'd gone, they'd taken their revenge, so why did you go back to them?"

"Because of you." Then he sighed, readjusting his position to turn more towards me. "They were under the impression you were in the car too. You were meant to be, but you'd come down with a fever and had stayed at home with me instead. It took three days to get the car out of the water. I used that time to get you into hiding and to disappear from what had been our lives up until that point so everyone we knew would think we were dead. By that time the Polzins knew the truth – that you were still alive.

"They started searching for you, putting the pressure on me, and I agreed to go back if they stopped looking. I would gladly have died at that point. Losing your mother was devastating, but I had to stay alive to look after you, even if it was at a distance."

"How did you find Ben and Lisa so quickly?"

"I didn't. I already had them in place as a safe house. I'd been planning for you both to go and live with them for a while, but I messed it all up, got the timing wrong."

"So there was a change of plan."

"Yes. I showed up with only you, we renegotiated, and they took you in."

"And you thought it was better for me to grow up thinking I was all alone and staying with random people rather than being put into foster care where I might have had the chance of being adopted and settled?"

"Yes, I did at the time. I know it was selfish, Emma, but I always intended on getting you back once I could sort things out with the Polzins properly. I didn't realise the consequences. I had to make a split-second decision, and that was the choice I took. Once made I couldn't take it back. You couldn't suddenly pop back up again, alive and well and as if nothing had happened."

I could see that. "What made everyone else believe we were dead?"

"As soon as I heard of the accident, we left. Literally we walked out of the door in what we had on. I had a bag packed for such an emergency. To anyone coming round the house it was like we'd just stepped out for a while, intending on coming back shortly. As it was, it was three days before the police came to the house to try to find us. They couldn't come round any earlier because they didn't know whose car it was until it could be brought to the surface. By then the trail was cold, and they didn't bother looking any further anyway believing instead that we'd all been in the car.

"The car was a soft top and that was ripped off on impact. Divers were sent down to search for us, but when nothing was found it was assumed our bodies had been washed away down river. The official conclusion to the investigation was that I'd probably tried to get you out and we'd both died in the process. Case closed."

What a way for our lives to change forever. The room was silent and I realised that, although it was Volkov and I who were having the conversation, everyone else was listening. It was probably just as well; it would save having to go over everything again later.

"So what happened next?"

"I think you know the rest, Emma. I arranged a series of homes for you. I had to keep you moving to make sure the Polzins never got a hint of where you were. I relocated your 'foster' parents each time as soon as you left them, set them up with new identities, all to cover yours. I couldn't risk the Polzins catching up with any one of them."

"That must have been expensive."

"I'm in a lucrative business." He glanced at his watch. "Sorry, Emma, but I need to be leaving now. It's getting late and I've probably given you more than enough to be thinking about for the time being. I'd like to come again, though, if you will see me. I'm sure there is more you want to ask."

There was, but right now my mind was on information overload and I needed some time to take it in.

"That would be fine," was all I was going to give him; I didn't want to appear too keen. We agreed he would be in touch when he could and left it at that. I pushed myself up off the settee, ignoring the proffered hand to help me up as he stood, and we walked up the office together. He prepared to leave after another round of hand shaking, mine included. I was pleased he wasn't suddenly expecting me to be all hugs and kisses. He left the way he had come, despite offers to drive him to wherever he wanted to go, and I wondered how he had got onto the estate as it hadn't been via either of the gates.

We had a debriefing when he'd gone, the general feeling being that he seemed genuine. Despite my misgivings over the way he'd handled things with me, over this I had to agree.

Trent and I didn't speak much on the way home. We checked the horses and topped up water buckets before going into the cottage, where we were greeted by an exuberant Susie who had been on her own far too long. She rushed outside to do her business then came back in for some cuddles, joining us on the settee.

Trent had poured himself a drink and brought a glass of water in for me. As he handed it over, he commented, "You're quiet."

"Hmm…"

"Should I ask how you're feeling about this?"

"No, because I don't know myself."

He wrapped his arm around me and pulled me in tight to his body, his hand on my stomach as he tried to feel Baby moving. Right then Baby wasn't playing ball.

"Talk to me, Em."

"Okay, but you're going to think I'm crazy."

"Really? Why?"

"I feel a bit deflated, actually. I'd ridiculously built up the notion that my mother might still be alive too, but she isn't, and...I don't know..."

"You didn't tell me that was what you were hoping for."

"Like I said, it was ridiculous. I thought I'd better keep it to myself so you didn't think I was going mad, but stupidly now I feel disappointed. Though my thoughts are all jumbled up, Trent, there's too much going on in my head."

"So tell me, it will help straighten things out."

"Well why didn't he stay with me at the safe house instead of going back to them? We could have disappeared, gone into hiding, got new identities – clearly he had no problem sorting them out for all the 'foster' parents." I even did the air quotes. "So why not for us? I don't understand it. Nothing would ever make me leave my child, and yet he did."

"And you're angry with him?"

"Yes, and resentful. Wouldn't you be?"

"I think he had a tough choice, Em. We don't know why he felt the need to go back to them, you will have to ask him next time. I'm sure he had a good reason."

I leaned away and turned to look at him, knowing my face showed my surprise. "Why are you on his side?" I realised how childish that sounded.

"I'm not on his side, but I can see the position he was in, how difficult that would be."

"So – what? You'd leave your child?"

"I know you're spoiling for a fight, Emma, but you're not going to get one here so don't put words in my mouth. All I'm saying is you never know what you would do until you find yourself in the same situation. He seems like a decent guy and I'm sure he had good reason for doing what he did."

Trent pulled me back into his body and hugged me tight.

"Why are you always so damned reasonable?" I grumbled as I felt his soft chuckle in my ear. While I wanted to lie there cuddling, I couldn't quite let it go so sat back up and looked at him.

"Anyway, what do you mean 'he seems like a decent guy', Trent? He kills people," I remonstrated. He went quiet.

"And what is it you think I do, Emma?"

I thought for a moment. "I know sometimes you have done, but surely that's an…" and I searched for the right words, "…an unavoidable outcome to your mission. You don't get given a contract to go and kill someone deliberately."

Or did he? I'd said this more as a statement, but I found myself questioning what I thought I'd believed about him. He stayed quiet.

"Oh, I get it, you see yourself as some sort of kindred spirit with your new-found father-in-law, is that it?"

He shrugged, and I detected an edge of sulkiness to his response of, "We're not that different."

"You are nothing like him," I stated, wondering who I was trying to convince.

"If you say so, Emma," came his somewhat weary response.

Chapter 8

He arrived in the night a week or so later. We'd heard nothing from him, but got back from an early supper at the Manor and there he was in the kitchen.

Susie on his lap.

Traitor.

I jumped as I walked in, stopping in my tracks. Trent followed me in as Volkov stood, allowing Susie to drop to the floor where she shook herself, only then deigning to come and say hello.

Volkov held out his hand which Trent took.

Traitor.

"How did you get in here?" I demanded.

"You don't need to know, Emma."

I glared at him.

"You can't just go around breaking into places."

"I didn't break in, there's no damage."

"And what are you doing with my dog?"

"Ahh, Susie and I are old friends."

I scowled at her as Trent murmured close to my ear, "He's not the enemy, Em, play nicely." Walking in and finding him here had put my hackles up. Why couldn't he behave like a normal person and let us know when he was coming? And it irritated me that Susie was all over him, but I took a deep breath and tried again.

"If you took my number perhaps you could let me know when you're coming and I could be here ready for you." I recited my number. He didn't write it down or put it in a phone, a point I commented on.

"It's best I don't keep that information anywhere other than in my head."

"Will you remember it?" He recited it back. Okay then. He didn't offer me his number.

"Can I get you a drink, Volkov? Emma?" Trent asked as I led the way into the sitting room. Volkov and I sat on separate settees, and Trent followed us in with glasses and a bottle of bourbon. With everything that had happened over the last couple of weeks I'd never felt more like I needed a proper drink and sighed as Trent handed me my water.

I watched Volkov as Trent poured and handed a glass to him and thought of the conversation I'd been party to that morning. It was, I guess, a beautiful April morning, though I was struggling to see it. I hadn't been as bad as in previous years, but we'd just passed Eva's birthday again and it was a time I struggled through. Trent and I had gone to take flowers to her – daffodils.

It had been noticeable how the number of visitors to the stables had increased over the last week and I was sure the word had gone out for everyone to keep an eye on me. I was larger now and finding the work harder, having to soak my aching body in the bath at the end of each day, so Turner was there most days anyway giving me a hand. But if it wasn't Peters and Stanton working in the gardens then it was Porter arriving to take the pickup off for servicing, or Young and Burton coming to clean. Carlton and Greene came to ride out each day, and the school holidays had started so Sophia and Reuben were back. They had been over several times either to ride out with the others or spend some time with me in the arena.

That morning Mrs F had arrived with Bray and a box full of goodies that they'd kindly put together. They'd hustled into the kitchen and accepted coffees as I updated them on my recent doctor's check-up. There was little to report, but they always wanted to know every detail – and we kept off the subject of Eva.

Bray asked how I was feeling having met my father. I'd barely answered with "Confused" when Mrs F chimed in.

"Bray tells me he's very good-looking." And I'd glanced at Bray, astonished to notice her cheeks colouring as she told Mrs F to hush now in embarrassment. Bray was a widow, I knew that, and as I looked at Volkov now I could see why she would be attracted to him. But, although he was good-looking his blue eyes appeared haunted and there was a sadness about him that I suspected had been there since my mother had died, or possibly since he had started taking the lives of others. All that killing must sap the joy of living from your soul.

On top of all the activity and the emotions of the anniversary, I'd had to deal with the turbulent feelings caused by meeting Volkov. Things I hadn't thought about in years kept me awake at night and filled my mind with such turmoil I was struggling to deal with it. Susie knew I was on edge and stayed close, refusing to leave the yard now to go out for her walk with the others. Trent knew my state of mind from my tossing and turning in the night until eventually I'd give up on sleep and wander downstairs to read. Though then, unable to take anything in, I'd find myself with the book open, the words a blur before my eyes as thoughts churned over in my mind. Vicious, angry, hurtful thoughts gnawed at me as memories that I'd thought were closed away forever were woken and rose up in my conscious mind to torment me.

Memories of my childhood, when lonely and unloved, unwanted by anyone, I'd been moved on continually by those paid to care for me. And the thought that my father had been there all along, had been alive and yet hadn't chosen to be with me, inflamed my anger. Having lost a child, I couldn't imagine any reason why he would deliberately leave me to go back to the Polzins other than the fact he hadn't loved me. Not in the way I knew love to

111

be between a parent and a child: where you loved with a raw animal passion that you would never give up.

All in all it had been a difficult week. As I looked over at the man whom I perceived to be at the root of all my angst I couldn't help but feel a little peeved at him.

And I was understating that.

He raised his glass in a silent toast and we did the same, then after he'd swallowed most of the contents of the glass he asked how we were, the baby and I. He knew it had been a difficult week for me with it being Eva's birthday. I was surprised. I hadn't thought he'd keep track of such dates and I told him so.

He tilted his head to one side as he contemplated me for a moment.

"Emma, she was my granddaughter. I remember." Of course she was. I hadn't even thought of that connection. Her grandfather. He paused for a moment, then continued, "I see you left daffodils for her again." This time I felt my eyebrows rise with my surprise.

"You've been to see her?"

"Yes, I go whenever I am in the country." Despite all my misgivings a sudden wave of affection for him softened my attitude. He drained his glass and Trent leaned over to top it up for him. Then, after refilling his own drink, Trent got up and said he'd got some paperwork to deal with and would leave us to it for a while. Volkov inclined his head to him in silent thanks and Trent went through to the office.

"So, Emma, I'm sure you have many questions for me," he prompted and while I agreed I didn't know where to begin, deciding to tackle one major concern I had straight away.

"I've had many memories coming back to me over this last week, stirred up from who knows where, but I don't understand why I don't have any recollection of you at all, or my mother."

He shifted uncomfortably and looked away for a moment before giving me his full attention again. I sensed his indecision as to whether to tell me something or not.

"I promised you I would tell you the truth, Emma, so I will, but you may not like what I'm about to say."

There have been many things I haven't liked you saying, I thought; this looks like it's going to be another to add to the pile.

"Go on," I urged as I steeled myself for what was coming.

"You were only five remember, Emma. I couldn't risk you giving yourself away and I couldn't expect you to remember to only use your new name, so I…I arranged for you to be hypnotised to block out the memories you had…to forget your name…"

"Emma is not my name?" I spoke slowly, not able to believe what I was hearing. "You stole my name? And my memories?" We'd only just started our conversation but I could feel my anger rising already. I didn't even know my own name – how ludicrous was that?

"The memories are still there, Emma, somewhere buried deep. I'm told they can be triggered."

And then I remembered.

"Like with the box?"

That peaked his interest and he eagerly questioned, "Did it do that? Did it remind you?"

"Yes, well kind of. I caught the scent of something that reminded me of something, but I got no further than that."

"But you remembered about the hidden compartment?" I nodded as I thought back. I hadn't been aware of how I'd done it, but somehow I'd known it was there. I'd opened it so I must have done. Something jogged me, something I couldn't explain, but I knew it'd felt good.

"Your name…"

I looked up sharply and held my hand up. "No, I don't want to know who I should have been." I glared at him, daring him to continue, and I saw in his eyes the moment he backed down, though I sensed disappointment as I continued, "So I remembered the box, but not you. Is that not strange?"

"I think there has to be a trigger."

"And seeing you, meeting you, is not enough of one?"

"Apparently not." He sounded disconsolate. I didn't want to be antagonistic with my questions and wanting to know more I knew we needed some common ground to get us talking, so I went upstairs and picked up the box from where it had been living on my bedside table. Carrying it back downstairs, I sat next to him on the settee.

"I think it's time you talked me through these," and I opened the box to retrieve the photos. "What's the story with the box? Why would I remember it?"

He smiled, probably the warmest smile I had yet seen from him. "You loved playing with that box as a little girl. You were fascinated with the secret panel and we used to play a game where we would leave little gifts or notes in it for each other. You would draw me pictures, scribbles, your first attempts at your letters. Kisses...always kisses for me..."

His voice tailed off, the words misty, and he cleared his throat. "And if I was away and missed your bedtime I could look in there and you would have left me something. That showed me you loved me. I would do the same if I had to leave before you were up in the morning."

Oh...

I could feel the emotion in his words, and as he smiled at me his eyes shone. I looked away, back at the photos, and handed the first one to him. Me in my mother's arms.

"She was a beautiful woman." He sighed. "I feel guilty every day for what I did, for losing her, for leaving you without a mother." I knew what it was to live with guilt like that and I knew when you shouldered that burden it was seldom straightforward.

114

"You weren't the one who drove her off the bridge."

"It was my fault they were chasing her."

"That was their choice, their decision. Essentially all you did was leave a job. It might have been your fault that you got tangled up with them in the first place, but I don't think you should take the blame for everything that happened afterwards. There are those who should feel guilty for killing her and they will get their comeuppance. But I don't believe you are among those guilty."

"Thank you, Emma." I could hear the relief in his voice, the release of tension. "That means a lot." I smiled and handed him the next photo and asked him to talk me through it. Then the next, then the next…

We talked for another hour and then it was time for him to go. I walked out with him to the kitchen and he turned to me, awkwardly starting to say goodbye. I don't know what made me do it but I held my arms out to him and, with a look of relief, he walked right into them. My arms went around him, his body solid and spare, and I inhaled the masculine scent mixed with the smoke of the cigars I'd seen in his pocket – the scent I'd recognised from the box, warm and comforting. Closing my eyes, I relaxed into the security and safety of my father's arms as they enclosed me. Crushing me to him, he hugged me ferociously – and that was the trigger…

Something between a cry and a sob escaped from me, painfully, and I felt his body heave with unexpressed emotion. For a few brief moments I was transported back; a little girl again in his arms.

A wave of emotion threatened to engulf me as I heard him whisper, "Oh, Emma, I love you and I've waited so long…too long to tell you."

But overwhelmed, I couldn't respond.

Chapter 9

That hug well and truly mixed me up and I kept to myself as I tried to straighten the thoughts in my mind. I'd loved it actually and wished I could just accept it for what it was: my father back in my life. Let it go at that. I was envious of everyone else's apparent easy delight at Volkov coming forward and claiming me as his own – a fact that had now been proven by the results of the DNA test – but I couldn't. I felt uneasy. I knew I was angry with him for leaving me, resentful for him not choosing me, not staying with me and leaving the Polzins far, far behind, but there was something else. Something I couldn't yet put a name to was making me anxious.

We were all called up to the Manor a few evenings later for a meeting, and as I walked in the office the atmosphere was buzzing. I saw Trent across the room, the first time I'd seen him since he'd left the cottage that morning.

And then I saw *him*.

Volkov was there, and there wasn't a person on the estate that didn't want the chance to meet him. Apparently he was quite well thought of in the circles that everyone else here moved in – a celebrity of the shadowy underworld of assassination, if you will. Of course, until now no one had known what he looked like, and I guessed the secrecy and intrigue had added to the mystique of the man.

I wondered then if any of them were a tad disappointed to find that, when it came down to it, he was just a man after all, and one in his fifties at that. I imagined many who had heard tales of his vigilante-style killings had

116

envisaged him in some caped crusader get-up and were maybe feeling more than a little let down as he stood among them in an everyday checked shirt and jeans like any other mortal. Though I had to say, disappointment wasn't the feeling I got from the room.

I realised I'd been a bit up and down over the last few days, but right at that moment I was on a down and feeling pretty pissed off, mostly because Volkov hadn't been in touch with me. He hadn't told me he was coming so I didn't know until I walked in the office. I presumed he'd somehow made contact so Cavendish must have known, and Trent, but no one had seen fit to tell me. This meeting was all business, I was told later, although Trent apologised for not saying something, his excuse being it was last minute and he'd assumed Volkov had done so. Why he would assume Volkov was about to start considering my feelings was beyond me.

I halted momentarily as I walked in, realising what was going on as Volkov met my eye through the crowd and smiled as he raised his hand. I raised mine in return and carried on to the end of the room to see Trent. If Volkov was disappointed I didn't run up to him seeking his attention he didn't show it, and I told myself those days were well and truly gone. I guess he might have been hurt I hadn't been a little more welcoming, but like I said, I was all over the place.

Trent told me Volkov was here to discuss the latest on the Polzins and what we could do to flush them out and it was the ideal time for everyone to be updated on the situation. For some reason I was feeling lonely in the crowd so I wandered off to take my seat, making myself comfortable. Trent came and sat on the arm of the settee next to me, and everyone else started to settle down. Within a couple of minutes the room was quiet.

There was nothing formal about this meeting. After a brief introduction by Cavendish, Volkov was invited to give us an update, but it didn't appear to me he had much more to say than we already knew. Anatoly and Orlov were still keeping themselves out of the action and it was pretty much impossible to pin down where they were as they moved so regularly.

I realised that not everyone on the estate had heard all of this already so it was bringing them up to speed, but I started to wonder what the point was of me being at this meeting. My train of thought was wandering off in quite another direction when the reason was suddenly made brutally clear.

Volkov had told us he would be given until mid-April to complete the contract. That had been a week ago and while he'd received no pressure from the Polzins he was understandably anxious about the delay and felt we needed to do something else to draw them out.

Carlton asked what form that 'something else' might take. Volkov paused for a long moment, and I knew as soon as the words left his mouth that this was what he had come to tell us. This was the whole purpose of the meeting. He weighed his words carefully before speaking.

"It would take them finding out who Emma really is."

The room erupted and Trent was on his feet immediately, striding towards Volkov as he responded sternly, "No, you are not using her as bait."

I sat in silence as I watched the chaos unfold around me, everyone talking at once. Cavendish trying to reason with a furious Trent, telling him they were sending people after me anyway. If they knew I was Volkov's daughter they might just come themselves.

I knew right then what I needed to do. I hated being dependent on anyone else but whilst I was vulnerable because of my physical state now was not the time for me to be weak. While it went against the grain, I was going to have to accept help and put my trust in others. Grabbing the arm of the settee, I pulled myself forward and stood, watching those around me arguing about how best to protect me. They were willing, and I hoped they were right.

I caught Volkov's eye and held it as I said, "Let them come."

My voice was nowhere near loud enough to be heard by all, but those immediately around me hushed, the ripples flowing outward to reach Trent and Cavendish, who were still arguing. Aware of the silence building around them, though unaware of its cause, they also became quiet.

Trent turned towards me. "Did you say something, Emma?" I could hear in his voice that he half suspected, but didn't want to believe.

"I said let them come, Trent." And I watched his face cloud with pain as he closed his eyes briefly. "This vendetta of theirs has already been going on most of my lifetime. They killed my mother and it's time it was ended, one way or another."

I looked around the office at all my friends before continuing, "I'm sorry you've all been dragged into this, but what was your business anyway has been made personal and we might as well take advantage of that opportunity if we can. Orlov's need for vengeance is his weakness and it will be their undoing. If it takes me to be the one to draw them out then so be it. Let them come."

I could see the fury in Trent's eyes, but it was mixed with something else and I hoped I recognised it right: pride.

The meeting was winding up and the room gradually emptied. I was tired and, making my excuses to go, I went to say goodbye to Volkov, which was awkward and stilted after our hug the last time we'd left each other. But he didn't seem to want to push it by expecting another one with everyone around and I appreciated that. I told Trent I was off home and he told me he'd join me as soon as the meeting was fully wrapped up.

When I left the room I needed to go to the toilet first – big baby, small bladder and all that. I went to the same one I'd visited the night of the 'big interrogation'. As I walked back towards the office I saw the door had been left open, and I slowed my pace as I could hear Volkov's voice clearly. I stopped – something in the urgency of his tone made me and, standing as close to the doorway as I could without giving myself away, I shamelessly eavesdropped.

Obviously I had no idea what the lead-up conversation had been, but Volkov was earnest in the way he was speaking. I heard, "…you know what he is like, what he is capable of, Trent. Whatever it takes…You do understand me, don't you? I'm relying on you when I say that…"

Trent's simple response – "I understand" – sounded serious and loaded with resignation to whatever was being asked of him, then I heard footsteps approaching. I swiftly pushed myself off the wall and walked away from the office so I was not in the vicinity by the time Cavendish reached the door. As I glanced back I saw him peer out, but he didn't spot me. Then he pushed the door closed.

I walked back past the office door, not bothering to look in and let Trent know I was heading to the stables, assuming I'd meet him there later. I didn't even get as far as the kitchen before Greene caught up with me, closely followed by Carlton, and they offered to take me home.

From that moment on I knew I was being guarded. Nothing was obviously said, but when we got back to the stables, Turner was there unnecessarily doing the late watering. I could have done that, but everyone was keen to get me into the house. The three of them came in for a coffee then left when Trent got back a short while later.

He was twitchy and unsettled and, I thought, pissed off at me for offering myself up so easily to lure Orlov here.

"Are you angry with me?" I decided I'd better just come out and ask to get it over with.

"What do you think?" His response, initially fierce, surprisingly tailed off as he grabbed the back of one of the kitchen chairs with both hands. Bowing his head low, he groaned in what sounded like frustration. "Why did you have to do that, Emma?"

I didn't think I needed to answer. Suddenly he let go of the chair, led me through to the sitting room and sat me down, taking both my hands in his and looking at me earnestly before surprising the hell out of me.

"I'm thinking perhaps we should leave the estate."

"What?" was my stunned reply. I'd never seen him this rattled.

He shook his head. "This is not going to end well, Emma, I can feel it, and I want you away from here, somewhere safe." I stared at him in disbelief. It had always been me that had got itchy feet in the past and been the one to consider leaving. Where would we go? My house in Crowthorpe was still occupied so that was out of the question, and anyway, Volkov knew about that so you could bet the others would before too long. We could just go and hide out in some hotel or bed and breakfast somewhere, but what would that achieve? Our problem was not going away. It had to be dealt with however much we didn't want to.

"We can't leave now, Trent, we need to bring an end to this. Everyone's ready...it will be fine." I tried to reassure him though, like him, I wasn't so sure. Although I wanted to question him about what I'd overhead, I couldn't because of the circumstances in which I'd gained the knowledge. He was holding something back, I knew it. Something was going on between him and my father, but he didn't open up.

I knew he wasn't convinced by my assertions that all would be well, but before we could take it any further a distraction arrived in the form of a text from my father. My first. He'd sent:

'Am sorry we had no time together like the other night, as it gave me great pleasure that you went through the family photos with me. Maybe another time, as it was lovely to see you this evening. X'.

It was something – actually it was more than something, it was a good start. Caller ID showed his number to be withheld so I could do nothing to encourage or extend the contact, but he'd listened.

I showed it to Trent who studied it for a few moments, making some sort of non-committal noise as I told him about it being a good start. His eyes narrowed in thought before he handed me back my phone and agreed with me that it was indeed a start. I wasn't convinced he was sincere. He was distracted and I believed only saying what I wanted to hear, but I wasn't sure what was behind that belief. He'd moved on from wanting to leave, however, not returning to the subject as we got ready to go to bed.

When I let Susie out I saw Wade and Hayes sitting in a pickup out in the yard. Another pickup was parked in front of the cottage, though from the bedroom window I couldn't see who was in that one.

"Is this entirely necessary?" I murmured to Trent as we got into bed. "Volkov's only just left. It's hardly likely the Polzins are going to strike in the middle of the night, are they?"

"Who knows, Em? We don't know where they are, or how quickly Volkov will tell them, or how quickly they'll move after that – if they move at all. Best be prepared." I lay on my side, his body curved around mine, his arm holding me closer as his hand rested comfortably on my breast. I could feel his chest up against my back, his skin warm, and I smiled.

"Meanwhile we've just got to sit and wait?" That thought was an uncomfortable one and I sounded impatient.

"Yes, but you know how it is, Em. With our lives in danger, we need to make the most of every second, for any moment could be our last." I didn't need to be able to see his face; I could feel his smile as he continued, his voice humming through me, "I think we should try to distract ourselves, fill the time as best we can."

I felt him lean up behind me, his hand skimming its way up my leg, over my hip, my waist, reaching for my breasts, my nipples, his lips finding their way up my neck, his teeth grazing my earlobe as I turned towards him – though not as easily as I'd managed to a couple of months before. This part of our lives had become more of a logistical challenge the larger I'd grown. Now we fitted together whichever way we could manage, and tonight Trent sat up and reached to pull me astride him, our baby cradled between us. I hoped among all the anxieties being filtered through to him, Baby would also feel our love for each other.

Trent's hands were restless on my thighs, then, moving to my hips, they held me tighter, guiding me as I rose up on my knees before lowering myself on to him. As he hitched his hips, thrusting into me, I slowed him, my hand on his chest where I could feel his heart pounding. His lips, his tongue were on my breasts, and I marvelled at the way the changes in my body hadn't put him off, not one little bit. He'd told me he was making the most of me, all of me, while he could, and I loved that. He turned me on just saying it. He looked up, meeting my eyes as I leaned in to kiss him, his mouth soft and gentle, his tongue teasing and flicking, meeting mine then stilling as I took his into my mouth sucking on it, toying with it then releasing it only to feel his desperation for more.

I pushed him back so I could lean forward, sinking lower onto him, the slick heat of my need for him deliciously taking every inch and as I did I felt his temperature rise, beads of sweat breaking across his forehead as I held him. I moved slowly, directing the pace, holding him back from taking more as his body strained beneath me, seeking its release, my body imploring for the same, my desire eventually giving it to him harder, faster, just what he wanted, our kisses harsh, our mouths absorbing each other's cries as we came…

In the early hours it became clear to me. Having taken a long time with all the chaos that was percolating through my brain, I finally realised what it was, the reason for my disquiet. In the end it was quite simple: I didn't believe Volkov would put me first. I didn't believe a man who could walk away from his child, leaving it to be brought up by strangers, would choose me over the people who paid him, the people who had run his life for so many years.

In short, I didn't trust him.

I couldn't shift this thought from my mind so lay awake for hours and the sleep that eventually came was so close to being awake it didn't deserve the name.

The lack of a decent night's rest made for an overly tired start to the day which when coupled with the fact that my generally peaceful yard was overpopulated didn't help my grumpy state of mind.

I prepared the horses for their rides and watched them leave, longing to get back to being the one taking them out; then I mucked out, filled water buckets and hay nets, swept the yard and groomed all four of my charges when they returned. And throughout there was a steady flow of people checking in to see that everything was all right and being terribly casual about it which made me more edgy than ever as it was obvious that actually no, everything was not all right.

But as we always do in these situations, I assured everyone who stopped by that everything was fine and we smiled and chatted about nothing, rather than facing up to the truth of what was coming.

Ridiculously, considering who had been the cause of me feeling like this, I was pleased to receive a couple more texts from Volkov. The first, just after breakfast read:

'Good morning, I trust you had a peaceful night. X'.

The second, later on in the morning:

'I hope you're having a good morning and I look forward to seeing you again soon. X'.

Short but sweet. Once he'd started it appeared he couldn't stop but I appreciated it; perhaps one day our relationship could become something real.

I told Trent of my misgivings after lunch when we took Susie out for a walk. She had stopped going out on the first ride of the day ever since Volkov had turned up. Sensing my mood changes she didn't like to leave me so I'd generally take her out for a walk every day instead.

Now Trent insisted on coming with me and he'd made sure that others knew where we were and were reasonably nearby should they be needed.

I wanted to walk much further than Trent wanted me to. Naturally in his ideal world he would have liked me to remain in the cottage, preferably under lock and key, but I'd got my way by telling him I'd read that walking was good for getting the baby in the right place for delivery. I actually had no idea whether that was true or not, but it did help me get rid of some of my current anxiety issues if I kept moving, so I felt justified economising with the truth.

Walking through the woods was therapeutic for my rattled nerves. Now that we were getting towards the end of April the estate was fully cloaked in spring. Fresh vibrant greens surrounded us, the tree canopy above filled with the restless urgency of nesting and new birth. Exhausted parents, in their endless quest for food, criss-crossed the woods to satisfy hungry mouths. Squabbles broke out sporadically over mates, nesting sites and food, the competition heightened at this frantic time.

The ground was richly covered in new growth too and I was delighted to see the first bluebells out, knowing that within days more would follow to roll out a blue carpet across the woodland floor, filling the air with their heady scent. It was getting warmer, certainly when out from under the trees, though here we were shaded from what spring sunshine there was around and I was pleased I'd pulled on my jacket as we'd left.

"So do you think I'm justified not to trust him?" I challenged Trent, wondering if he'd defend Volkov again.

"Well he sounded pretty genuine last night," he replied.

Of course he did, it's all an act, I thought.

"What he's doing is pretty dangerous, Em. He's got to accidentally let slip who you are to the Polzins, a secret he's managed to keep to himself for more than twenty-five years. How he's going to do that without it looking suspicious I don't know, and then he's somehow got to build it up enough to make Anatoly and Orlov come after you without them thinking they're walking into a trap."

A text came into my phone. Caller ID showed the number to be withheld and I found myself surprised by the small thrill of anticipation elicited by getting a message from Volkov.

"Oh, another one, he's getting prolific," I exclaimed, as Trent's phone went.

Only it wasn't from him.

"What do you mean 'another'?" Trent asked, speaking quickly, as he answered his call.

It read:

'We know who you are, Emma, see you very soon.'

Icy water trickled down my spine as my hair prickled on my scalp in alarm. I stood frozen, staring at the message. I watched him, as he listened to the call and then went still. I saw his eyes flick over to me then away as he cast his gaze around the woodland. I held up my message to him, saw his eyes widen as he relayed it to whoever had called. I suspected it was Cavendish.

"There have been others?"

I nodded and Trent took my phone from me, scanning through the messages and reading them to the caller, then after listening for a few moments confirmed his agreement to whatever was being said and finished by saying we were heading for the tree house.

"What about the messages?" I demanded.

"Only the first one was from Volkov."

"How do you know?"

"Code. No time to explain now. A party of five has been spotted on the estate in the stable yard." Pausing briefly, he added with reluctance, "Volkov is one of them."

Well of course he was. I wasn't surprised and I didn't bother saying I told you so. I was pretty certain my expression spoke volumes. He'd brought them straight here and got them onto the estate. I couldn't believe they'd come so quickly, though. I'd imagined a few days, not less than twenty-four hours.

"What now?" was all I could manage as I suddenly realised how exposed we were; how defenceless I was.

"Now," he looked at me, his expression serious, "we run."

Easier said than done when you were the size I was, but I did my best. Moving any faster than a walk was uncomfortable so I held on to my stomach as we doubled back and headed cross country for the tree house, which was situated between us and the stables. I'd been diligent in working out at the gym, but that was not enough to counteract the effects the late stages of pregnancy can have on a body. Trent scooped Susie up as we passed her, doing his best with one arm wrapped around me to help me along. It was hard going. Leaving the paths meant rougher undergrowth to negotiate and the ground was naturally hillier this side of the estate. Cumbersome, I found myself tripping and stumbling down banks and struggling to get up the inclines on the other side.

Fear was the driver, a desperate need to get under cover. Fortunately it wasn't too far, which was just as well as I was gasping for breath, my body shaking by the time we stood at the edge of the clearing from where we could see the house built into the branches of three large trees. We stopped for a moment as Trent checked the coast was clear, then we crossed the horribly exposed area to the stairs, which we ran up. Or rather, Trent ran up them and I lumbered behind as he dragged me along with him, pulling keys out of his pocket at the same time, throwing the door open and me inside as fast as he could.

Chapter 10

Trent closed the door, plunging us into near darkness. Chinks of light showed around some of the shutters that guarded the windows. He put Susie down on the floor as I collapsed onto one of the kitchen chairs, my body hot, sweating and heaving with the exertion of the run. I noted Trent was barely out of breath while my lungs felt like they were on fire. I took a few moments, gradually steadying my breaths, eventually able to take longer, more controlled ones. Even after such a relatively short period of exercise my body was complaining, my joints feeling loose and weak. I sat forward, trying to ease the ache in my back as I leaned on my knees, calming my trembling body.

Cracking one of the shutters a fraction, Trent peered out, still and quiet. Presumably satisfied with the outside world, he glanced over at me.

"You okay?" I nodded, trying to get my breath back. His attention had returned to the window. "We could be here for a while. Why don't you go and lie down for a bit? Try and make yourself comfortable."

"Okay," I replied, attracted by that idea. "Can you make sure the cat flap is closed first?" I didn't want Susie wandering back outside. My eyes had grown accustomed to the dark and I could now see the outlines of furniture and doorways. I stood, using the table to push myself up and off the chair, and as I did I felt the strangest sensation. A pop, deep, deep inside. I hesitated a moment – nothing else – and let out my held breath.

And then it began: the long, slow building of a contraction, my belly hardening like with the practice ones

I'd experienced, only this felt different. Rippling and purposeful. Deep inside I could feel the muscles working, peeling me ever so slightly open, the tiniest trickle of water between my legs making adrenaline spike through my veins as my arms and legs weakened and my hand clamped on the table for support.

Oh no, no, no…not now…

As the contraction ebbed away, instead of heading for the lie down I wanted in the sitting room, I turned and went to the bathroom, grabbing a towel from the pile next to the basin on the way. I dropped my jeans and pants and sat on the toilet, anxious about what might happen next.

I was right to be concerned. There was none of the 'five minutes between contractions' nonsense; I'd barely sat down when the next one started. Stronger than the first, it meant business.

The 'pop' had been my waters breaking, and the strength of this contraction meant that I was highly relieved to be where I was as they gushed out of me. I took a couple of deep breaths as the contraction subsided. My body felt like it was being taken over and shook with the shock of what was happening to it. The good news? Not too much pain…yet.

The next contraction came and went, stronger again and definitely taking more of my attention, but most of the water appeared to have already been expelled. Using the towel as a just-in-case measure, I pulled up my jeans and went to break the news.

I'd barely opened the door when the next wave struck. I grabbed hold of the door frame as I curled over with the discomfort this one caused. "Trent," I gasped.

Unable to breathe and speak at the same time, I couldn't answer as he muttered, "What is it?" from his vantage point. When he didn't receive an answer I saw him glance in my direction, his eyes widening as he took in my condition, but as if frozen he stayed mute.

The contraction eased and I was able to reply, "The baby is coming." Although it felt like I was stating the bleeding obvious, I said it anyway. He looked aghast, his response equally unnecessary.

"But you're not due for another couple of weeks."

So true, but hardly relevant now, and my reply was a little arsy.

"I realise this is inconvenient…"

He left his station by the window and crossed the room to me. "Okay…" He took a deep breath and blew it out, as if to steady his own nerves at this turn of events. "Okay, we'll get you to hospital. I'll arrange a car…no, I'll get an ambulance here."

He went to call, but my hand closed over his.

"We can't call an ambulance – it would draw too much attention, and…" I could feel another contraction coming and as it built I lost concentration on what I was saying, only able to cope by breathing through it, then as it receded, "…it will put others in danger." I was breathing heavily as I moved towards the bedroom. Trent's arm went around me in support and I heard his small groan as I told him the even worse news.

"Anyway I'm sorry, Trent, but I don't think there's any time for us to get to hospital. Baby's coming too fast."

"What? You're going to have it here?" I could hear the note of panic in his voice. "How the hell are you going to do that? We don't have everything you need to have a baby."

"We'll have to make do, we have no choice, and unless…you have…someone…out there…qualified…" the contraction peaked before I could continue, "…as a midwife…it's going to be down to us."

He peered round the dark room as if for inspiration. When he next spoke he was considerably more reassuring. "Okay, okay, we can do this," and I was relieved to hear him sound like he was taking charge, right when I needed him to.

We needed more light and as I took off my jeans and climbed onto the stripped-down bed Trent carefully opened one of the shutters an inch, checking the coast was clear before opening it fully. He did the same with a couple of others then looked back at me.

"Let's hope nobody notices. I need to get some cover in place. See if I can get hold of Stanton, possibly Lawson. Will you be all right for a moment?"

"Yeah, can you make sure Susie doesn't come in?" Agreeing, he left the room. I could hear him talking quietly in the kitchen, but another contraction came and, totally focused on that, I heard nothing of what he said. It was clouding over outside, the sky darkening. I could see the first splashes of rain on the windows, hear the patter on the roof, but having some shutters open improved the light levels in the room considerably.

While my head was clear for a moment I thought through what we might need, only sparing a moment to think longingly of the case I'd packed with the essentials, now standing uselessly by the back door at the cottage.

This will be fine, I told myself. Women do this all the time, and it wasn't as if I hadn't done it before. This was very different, though. I'd been in labour with Eva for hours – though it had felt like days, days of unrelenting waves of contractions. This time I could feel things were moving fast. Last time I had pain relief, the joys of gas and air to see me through. This time there would be nothing, and the fear that thought evoked ran through me as sweat pinpricked my skin. I shivered as the first wave of panic hit me.

"Trent," I sobbed as loudly as I dared. He appeared almost immediately in the doorway, just pocketing his phone, and rushed round to the side of the bed. He held my hand tightly as the next contraction was already overwhelming my senses, though I could hear him, his words soothing, comforting, as though to a wounded animal. As it passed this time, I knew I had to get some things organised. I looked over at him.

"Have you sorted the cover out?"

"Yes, Cavendish has kept a guard in place at the Manor and sent everyone else over. They're going to surround us, at a distance so as not to draw attention, but close enough to make sure no one gets through to us. Stanton and Lawson are on standby, but at a safe distance for now. I don't want to risk them coming any closer unless it is absolutely necessary."

"I need you to get a few things. We'll have to manage the best we can with what we've got." Then I couldn't speak any more as the next contraction rolled through me. Each one was stronger than the last and I couldn't help but moan softly at the pain of this one. As it passed I regained control of my breathing and looked at Trent.

"Go to the kitchen drawers and find some scissors and see if there's some string or something like that in there, then get as many towels as you can find."

"All right." Then he didn't move. "Emma?"

"Yes?"

"You're going to have to let go of my hand."

Oh, I really didn't want to do that.

"Okay, but hurry back." And as soon as I let go, he sprang away from the bed and rushed out to the kitchen. I heard mumbled curses and drawers being flung open as he searched through the contents for what he needed. Give him his due, he moved fast. After making a quick detour via the bathroom, he was back in no time with his bounty.

He grabbed my hand again as another contraction hit. Though I tried to relax against the pain, I could hear myself whimpering. I knew I couldn't risk making a noise that might be heard by our enemy. True they were unlikely to hear that, but once I got going who knew what might come out of my mouth? As soon as I could speak again, I muttered, "Pass me a small towel. I need to bite down on something."

At my urging Trent spread a few of the towels under me. We were about as ready as we were ever going to be and I tried to think through how this was likely to go. It was difficult though. My experience having Eva had been so different, and not only because it had happened safely in a hospital, surrounded by knowledgeable, reassuring midwives with the latest equipment to hand in case anything went wrong. But whenever I thought back to her birth I couldn't remember too much about it. I was exhausted by the time she'd actually arrived, deadened and pretty much out of it from all the pain relief I'd needed to get that far, and I had been totally in the hands of the midwives.

This time there was going to be none of that. This was probably going to be about as raw and primitive as it got in this country, I guess other than if I'd been outside. Thank goodness for small mercies.

The next contraction built, stronger again, the world slowing around me as I concentrated on the unrelenting wave of intensity crashing through my body. I tried to relax against the pain, but that was so hard, my body tensing instead as I tried to control my breathing, alternating between letting out long slow breaths and biting down on the towel to stop me from screaming when the pain level peaked. As the contraction began to subside, my thoughts, the room around me and Trent close by, holding my hand, soothing me, became clearer again.

"Can I do anything?" he asked, his anxiety clear in his expression.

"No." I shook my head, knowing I'd only have moments before the next wave struck. I could already feel my stomach starting to tighten, having barely finished from the last time. But this time was different: for the first time I got the urge to push. But I didn't. I panted, willing it to pass. I'd forgotten this. Last time the midwives had held me off from pushing too early, even though my body cried out to do so, wanting me to wait until I was ready. And now I panicked. I didn't know what to do. How would I know if I was ready or not? This contraction had subsided, but I knew the next one was going to mean business.

"I wanted to push that time. I don't know if I'm ready, Trent. How will I know?" My words choked as tears stung my eyes and my throat tightened. Fear flooded my senses, fear of what was coming next, my body shaking as I clawed at the bed with my free hand, desperation settling in as realisation struck as to the hopelessness of my situation. How could I do this seemingly impossible task? There was no way I was going to be able to get this baby out.

"Emma, look at me." Trent's voice was deep and calming. "Look at me." I turned my head and he fixed his eyes on mine. He took my other hand. "Stay with me, Em, you can do this. Listen to what your body is telling you. If you want to push, do it. I'm right here."

My muscles started tightening powerfully, wave upon wave now building to a peak, the urge to push coming again. Biting down hard on the towel, I tightened my grip on Trent's hands and, with my eyes never leaving his, I pushed down hard. I held my breath as I pushed, then gasped for air as the pressure began to ease. I felt movement, felt myself opening; with Baby a little nearer to edging out into the world my confidence buoyed just for having got this far.

"Okay?" Trent's eyebrows arched in question.

I nodded, saving my breath. Despite the intimacies we'd shared, it was awkward having to ask, and I was still breathing heavily as I did: "Could you check down there? See if you can see anything?" I didn't want him to look, but I needed to know. I needed to have some encouragement that I was getting somewhere. He looked, and came back to me, smiling.

"I can see the top of the head, Em, dark hair." I tried to smile because that confirmed what I already knew. I fixed on his face, his beautiful face. A contraction building again, the intensity increasing.

"Okay, this time I'm going for it. We have to get her out."

He caught on immediately. "Her?" I saw his tears brim as he smiled. "Come on then, Em, hold on tight. We can do this." He gripped my hands hard, meaning business, giving me something solid to cling to as I disappeared into the layers of pain. They engulfed me, building and building and building in a crescendo, reaching a peak of pain as I gathered every last ounce of strength I had and pushed down hard. Trent's eyes stayed focused on mine, his words of encouragement mouthed but not heard; it was as if I'd entered another plane of existence…

I saw her.

I knew who was coming.

I'd always known.

I'd seen her in my dreams before, but had been unable to tell anyone in case it was taken as a fanciful notion. Our little girl. I didn't see her as a baby, but as a little girl. I saw her as a two-year-old, standing in her nursery at the cottage, dark curly hair, piercing blue eyes, and right behind her this time was my Eva, forever six, smiling and encouraging her little sister forward as if to meet me. Then Eva looked up at me, smiling, her eyes never leaving mine. She was right there with me in this other world and I knew she was all right.

I pushed down hard and then there was nothing else.

Time stopped.

There was no Trent.

No tree house.

No estate.

No enemies.

Only me.

And my world stood still, suspended as if the universe had contracted, every star converging into a tiny pinprick of time and space, and all of it, *all of it* compressed in that one single moment and concentrated on me. My body screamed with the intensity of the pain, but I bit down harder and turned those screams inward, willing them on and pushing them down and into the very core of my body. I gave it everything I had, not wanting to have to go through another contraction; not knowing if I *could* go through another one.

And then...and then...the reward for my hard work. Barriers thrown aside as one clear hanging note of searing agony claimed me, a pain so sharp it took my breath with its ferocity, leaving in its wake churning waves that gradually receded. My body left a trembling wreck with the exertion as my surroundings came back into focus. Breathing heavily, I blinked at a shocked-looking Trent.

"Jesus!" he exclaimed, leaning in to kiss my cheek. "That was incredible." He glanced down: "The head is out." I smiled weakly, knowing the job was only half done, and I was damned determined to complete it on the next contraction, not knowing if I'd survive another after that. I barely had a moment, hadn't even caught my breath again before the next one was upon me, bearing down like a tidal surge.

"Get ready for her," I gasped, and this time we both looked down. I leaned up on elbows so weak they barely supported me but I had to see her. Trent released my hands and cradled her head in readiness. As the tension ripped through me again I tried to concentrate on the fact that this was going to be it, the last one, and aimed to gather myself in readiness, but I was too far gone for any kind of preparation. My thoughts scattered. My body, as if possessed, reacted to the forces of nature that controlled it as I felt the urge to bear down grow again. And I did, long and hard, making every effort to bring this new life out into the world. Pain peaked, but nothing like before. I breathed through it, focusing only on watching our daughter arrive. Once the shoulders were through, she slipped out into Trent's waiting hands and I collapsed back, exhausted and overwhelmed with relief. Complete and utter relief. It was over.

I took a moment to steady my breathing, to clear my head, and then I suddenly realised.

I couldn't hear anything.

Though this was a good thing in our situation, Eva had come into the world screaming. I pushed myself back up in alarm, experiencing the first, the very first of what I knew would be a lifetime of surges of anxiety that haunt every parent, every moment of every day.

But there she was, lying in Trent's hands, safe and well, jerkily stretching unused arms and legs into the unaccustomed space as she stared up at him. He in turn gazed back at her, transfixed. I watched him, unable to look away, his features softening, his heart melting as he fell completely, utterly and irrevocably in love with her. Tears sprang to my eyes.

"Hey…" I verbally nudged him softly back into the here and now. He looked over at me and I could only describe his expression as one of awe.

"You are amazing, Em. I never imagined…I never thought I would feel like this…"

I was thrilled for him, obviously, but my impatience was growing. I wanted to see her properly. I yearned to touch her, to hold her, to smell her, to feel the same as he did.

I smiled at him. "Can I?" Pushing myself back so I could lean against the ironwork of the bedstead I held my hands out towards her.

"Of course, sorry," and we rather clumsily transferred her from his hands to mine. She was warm and soft, though messy and wet. I was afraid of her slipping from me so I held her close and gazed down into blue eyes that stared back at me calmly. She was beautiful. I know every mother thinks the same, but she truly was. Dark hair covered her head, long enough that I could see the start of a curl to it. Daddy's girl. I smiled. A perfect little nose above rosebud lips and rounded cheeks like soft peaches. I felt it then, as I'd done once before: a feeling of contentment flooding through me, warming me, filling spaces that I'd known since losing Eva had been horribly empty. The feeling of complete fulfilment reassured me that this was going to be all right.

"Hello, Baby," I whispered, "we've been waiting to meet you for a long time." I looked over at Trent, who was watching me closely. He smiled too when he saw my big tearful smile. "Thank you for giving her to me."

He raised an eyebrow. "It was the least you deserved after all your hard work."

"No." I shook my head, wanting him to understand. "Thank you…for her…" and then he did.

"Anytime, Em," and he kissed me. Sadness and joy mixed in our tears until we parted, wiping our eyes. He grinned a little bashfully. "Do you think we should cut the cord?"

"Yes." While he reached for the scissors and string I organised her on my lap. I had no idea how this should be done and we had nothing sterilised or antiseptic that we could use, so Trent tied the string round the cord a little way from her belly then cut the cord above it. She was starting to get more active now and small mewling noises were coming out of her, so to avoid a full-scale cry possibly drawing unnecessary attention, I made myself a little more comfortable, opened my shirt, undid my bra and held her to my breast. Her head turned towards me and her mouth started seeking comfort. I remembered from Eva how to encourage her to latch on, which fortunately she did. After such a fast and relatively easy birth, Baby had been born full of energy – and with an appetite. I felt her drawing on the milk from my breast, which was a huge relief given our circumstances.

I'd already taken another towel and wrapped it around Baby's rear end, anticipating with her feeding that something was likely to start happening there, but I was also conscious of her getting cold.

"Can you sort out something to wrap her in? We need to keep her warm or she'll start crying." Trent went to check in the cupboard and came back with some more towels and a blanket which he cut in two.

"You know we don't have a name for her. What are we going to call her?" He sat watching me, I think half expecting me to have a name ready, but I didn't.

"I don't know. I couldn't allow myself to think we were going to have a girl so I seriously haven't thought of a name. We shall have to stick with Baby for a while longer."

"Sounds good to me." Then he excused himself and went to make some calls.

"We didn't distract him for long, did we," I murmured down at Baby, who had begun to lose interest in drinking any more. I cradled her as she lay contentedly full in my arms and thought through the practicalities of our situation, just as I knew Trent was doing. It would be better if we were with the others on the estate, and the Manor was the most secure place to be, so I thought we should head there. With that in mind I started making plans.

Sure enough, Baby had been rather unpleasantly busy. I started by cleaning her up as best I could, momentarily wishing again I had my case with me which would have made all of this so much easier. I fashioned a nappy out of a small towel and wrapped it around her. She was engulfed by it, but I tucked the ends in to make it as secure as possible. I took a larger towel, laid her on it and folded it across her one way then the other. It supported the back of her head, binding her arms close to her sides, and I enclosed it around her legs to give her as snug a feeling as possible before laying her on the bed beside me. She was a contented little thing, at least for the moment, and on the verge of falling asleep, which was good because I needed to sort myself out.

I only had my shirt covering up my dignity and had to get dressed if we were going to get out of here. I didn't seem to be bleeding too much so eased myself off the bed and tried to stand. It was at that point that I realised how exhausted my body was. My legs, as weak and wobbly as those of a newborn foal, struggled to hold me up; my body was battered, bruised and aching. I reached for my jeans and made my way to the bathroom, intending on using the facilities to clean up a little before dressing. I'd have loved nothing more than to have been able to sink into a warm soapy bath and pull on clean clothes after, but I was conscious of the time pressures and our need to get to safety, so I made do with stripping off and washing myself down to freshen up a bit. Feeling pretty feeble I had to clutch the edge of the basin a couple of times for support, but I knew there was no option other than to pull myself together and get ready to go. I used a towel again to protect against the aftermath of childbirth, tried to ignore the fact I felt like my insides were falling out and pulled up my jeans, which fortunately, being elasticated, stayed where they were despite there being no Baby to hold them up anymore.

141

I walked back into the bedroom, checked on Baby, who was now fast asleep, and pulled all the towels we'd used into a big bundle which I dumped in the bath. I then collapsed gratefully back onto the bed, my body feeling like it had run a marathon. I gathered Baby up into my arms, and as I watched her sleeping I wondered what Trent was up to.

He came back into the room a short time later with some water for me which I drank quickly, wiping my mouth with the back of my hand, not realising how thirsty I had been. He sat next to me on the bed, checking on Baby before he murmured, "Are you okay?"

"I'm fine." But now that the drama of Baby's arrival was over I was anxious about what was coming next. "What's going on outside, Trent? How are we going to get out of here?"

"It's all quiet at the moment, but we think they're still on the estate. We have no reason to believe they're not so I've enlisted some help in getting us back to the Manor." He hesitated, then, looking me fully in the eyes, he spoke carefully.

"Emma, please remember that what I do now I'm doing for the best of reasons."

I felt the ripple of apprehension run down my spine.

"What are you doing?"

I could feel him tense as he left my side. "You'll see in a minute." I watched him leave and wondered what he had planned. Whatever it was he already knew I was not going to be in favour of it.

I listened carefully now in case he made any calls, but instead I heard the front door open and close, hushed whispers, someone making a fuss of Susie. Then Trent appeared back in the doorway and I looked at him, waiting. He cleared his throat.

"Er, Em, I've brought someone to see you, to meet Baby," and he carried on into the room. I watched as

Carlton followed him in. My eyes flitted anxiously from one to the other. Something was up.

"Hi, Emma." Carlton spoke softly, as if wary of waking the baby, and acted as if he was cautious of approaching me with whatever it was he and Trent had cooked up. Then he came closer, bending over to feast his eyes on Baby's peaceful face for a moment before kissing me on the cheek. He sat on the bed facing me, casting a glance at Trent.

"Congratulations, you two, she's gorgeous. Emma, are you all right?"

"Thanks, Carlton, I'm fine." There was an awkward silence. I looked between him and Trent. "So, what is it you're not telling me?" I asked impatiently.

Trent inclined his head at Carlton, telling him to move out of the way. Trent took his place. "We need to get to the Manor, Em, and Carlton is going to take Baby there now…ahead of us."

"No," I said, "absolutely not. She stays with us."

"That's not the safest thing."

"I can't be separated from her, Trent."

He closed his eyes. "And I can't carry you both, Em."

"I don't need carrying."

"Yes, you do. You've only just given birth and we need to move faster than you're going to be capable of."

"Then we'll just stay here until it's safe."

"No, you need to get checked out medically, and we're splitting the manpower with us out here."

"Then let Carlton carry me. You take Baby."

I saw his jaw clench before he responded, "No."

"This is no time for you to be possessive, Trent. Carlton can take me."

"I'm not being possessive, Emma." He exhaled in frustration. "There's no easy way to say this but you're putting Baby in danger if you keep her with us. Orlov is after you first and foremost, then, to a lesser degree, me.

He doesn't know about her yet and we need to keep it that way. Don't you see, Emma? We have to put some distance between us and Baby to keep her safe."

And I did see. I saw it all now: I saw the choice my father had had to make in one moment of time oh so long ago, doing what he had to do in order to keep his daughter safe, putting the distance between him and me. Our situation now an echo of his from all those years ago.

Trent saw the realisation hit as I gasped, my hand coming to my mouth. He reached out to wrap me in his arms. "I know, I know," he repeated, murmuring softly as he rocked me.

"Oh my God, Trent, I didn't understand…and I've given him such a hard time."

"I know, but you can sort it out with him once this is all over." I nodded into his shoulder. I knew now exactly what I was going to have to do. Trent released me and I looked down at Baby. I couldn't believe I was going to let her go after everything I'd said, and although I knew Trent was right I still had some questions.

"Why is Carlton going to be alone? Why don't we get more people round her to protect her?" I thought it was a fair argument. Trent put his hand on mine, resting on top of Baby. I could feel his warmth.

"We believe we stand a better chance of getting Baby back to the Manor unnoticed if it is just one person. Carlton can move fast, doesn't have to rely on anyone else. He's our best option, Em." Then he went one step further. "He's had my back on more than one occasion. I trust him completely."

I glanced over at Carlton. "Come closer, I need to talk to you." Trent relinquished his place and sat on the chair nearest the bed, watching intently.

I couldn't believe I was going to do this, but I did know I would do whatever was needed to keep Baby safe, even if deep inside I still thought the safest place for her was with me. Who better to protect a child than their mother?

Carlton sat in front of me. "I have something to ask you, Carlton." I glanced over at Trent who confirmed his agreement. He knew what was coming. We had spoken of this, though never expected to be saying it in these conditions. "Firstly I want you to understand how precious Baby is to us."

"I do understand, Em." He was totally serious yet I didn't believe he had a clue – how could he? However, all I could do was continue on this track.

"Okay. This is the most important thing I will ever ask of you: if something happens to us we want you and Greene to bring her up as if she were yours, okay?"

He didn't hesitate. There was no need to ask Greene; he knew his partner, and he knew what she would say. "Of course we will, we'd be honoured."

I tried to smile, but there was more chance of tears coming now.

Carlton implored, "Emma, let me take her. Let me get her to safety. I'll look after her, and I promise whether it's for today, or forever, I will protect her..." I'd never seen him so serious as he placed one hand on his chest, "...with my life."

I nodded, not trusting myself to speak for a moment as I looked down into Baby's face and kissed her forehead. "Be a good girl for Carlton. We love you and we'll be back with you soon." Though she heard none of that, being fast asleep, I passed her into Carlton's waiting arms.

He leaned forward and kissed me on the cheek. "I love you, Em. See you soon, yeah?" That might have been inappropriate, but it felt good.

"Yeah, see you soon." I tried to sound more light-hearted than I was feeling but I was going to make sure it was *very* soon. Choking up, I watched Baby leave in Carlton's arms. Trent followed and I could hear them talking quietly in the kitchen for a few moments, then the door open and close again. They were gone.

I felt like crying but stifled my sobs. I needed to get after her and there was no time for me to fall to pieces now.

Trent came back in the room, all business. I watched him as he checked his gun, re-holstered it and got himself ready. I was anxious to get going, but he told me we had to wait at least ten minutes to allow Carlton to get away.

Ten minutes.

It was the slowest-moving ten minutes I ever remembered experiencing.

I would usually have paced during this waiting time, but with my body exhausted I tried to rest instead, needing to bring some energy back into muscles that had been wrung out of all their vitality.

And with anxiety overriding all my emotions I counted the minutes.

At long, long last it was time and Trent helped me off the bed and out into the kitchen. Susie came through from the sitting room where no doubt she'd made herself comfortable on the upholstery and I bent to give her a cuddle, feeling sadness wash over me again at the thought of having to leave her behind but knowing she would be safest here.

"We'll be back for you soon, Susie," I promised, hoping I was going to be able to keep it, suddenly nervous at the prospect of what lay in store for us.

Trent checked outside: everything was clear. He made a call, said, "We're coming out," and turned to me. "Ready?"

My throat was dry with fear and I swallowed with difficulty, my voice hoarse when I replied, "Yes."

"Come on, then," and taking my hand, he opened the door.

Chapter 11

Although my mind was set on the determined course of getting back to our baby as quickly as possible, my body was letting me down, being less able to do what I needed than I would have liked. All the strength had been sucked out of me, and as I struggled to put one foot in front of the other, overexerted muscles quivered. Going down the steps was the worst part and I used the railing to steady me, anxiously glancing around at the trees that surrounded us, keen to get out of this exposed area. Trent was equally eager to move on, and the minute I reached the bottom step he picked me up and carried me swiftly into the trees. His strength astounded me as he appeared to have no problem in doing this, and I was relieved he was able to.

The rain that had come since we'd arrived at the tree house had stopped but the temperature had dropped. Dank air enveloped us as soon as we stepped outside. As we reached cover, Turner fell into line with us on our right and Greene on our left. Both wore dark khaki fatigues, carried automatic type weapons and moved swiftly with us deeper into the woods. As we reached an area more thickly planted with trees we stopped and Trent put me down. I shivered, feeling the damp hanging in the air as droplets of water fell from the canopy above.

Trent steadied his breathing as he conferred with the other two on the latest intel. I listened as they discussed that we were going to stick to the cover of the woods, travelling away from the direction of the stables and round the estate to the back of the Manor. By that time it would be dark, or we would wait until it was dark – a wait I didn't like the sound of – before making the crossing over the open parkland to safety.

Then in a low voice Greene reported that Orlov's group had circled around those who had guarded us while I was giving birth. They were now somewhere on the route we were discussing taking to the Manor. That made no sense to me at all.

"Why don't we go the other way then? Towards the stables," I questioned, "rather than risk running into them?"

Trent placed his hands on my upper arms as if to hold me in place and laid it on the line.

"We're not going straight to the Manor. We have a job to do first. We have to find Anatoly and Orlov and deal with them." He spoke quickly, not allowing me to interrupt. "You brought them here, Em. You put yourself up as bait and now you have to see it through." It was blunt, to the point and, to be honest, took me by surprise, but it was needed. I'd been so focused on getting back to Baby I hadn't thought about what this situation meant for the rest of the estate.

"You mean…" I didn't even want to finish the question.

"I'm sorry. I know you want to get back to her, and we will, but first we're going hunting," Trent finished firmly.

"But why haven't they been dealt with by the others?" I waved my arm feebly in the direction of the surrounding trees, thinking our guards must be out there somewhere.

"Because they have collateral, and we need to at least try and get everyone out of this in one piece." I didn't understand what he meant, but it sounded like a final statement on the subject. I could feel it in his body language; mentally he was moving on, getting ready for the next challenge and I needed to as well. I shivered again and wrapped my arms around my body, holding myself together.

Trent checked in with each of us in turn, making sure our heads were in the right place for what might come. When he got to me I hoped I managed to look more confident than I felt.

"They are out there somewhere." He looked at each of us in the group. "*When* we come across them you know what to do." I didn't know what to do but stayed silent, fearing I would look stupid at my lack of woodland warfare knowledge. Trent filled in the blank anyway. "You follow my lead."

Trent quickly called Cavendish, who was with Sharpe watching the cameras. There had been no further updates on the intruders; they had crossed no other cameras, so if they were still here, and there was no reason why they wouldn't be, then they must be sticking to the woods. Volkov knew about the cameras attached to the Manor, and it was obvious he had informed those coming after me and they were avoiding going near them. I also knew he was aware of the ones that covered the stable yard. When he'd let himself into our cottage a few evenings ago he hadn't appeared on them – I'd checked with Sharpe, wanting to find out how he'd got in, but when the recordings were replayed there was no sign of him.

I therefore wondered why they had been spotted at the stable yard today, unless they didn't care if we knew they were there or not.

Trent picked me up again and we carried on. Having passed the initial rush of getting under cover, which had been done at as fast a speed as Trent could manage, he now slowed the pace to not much more than a jog, allowing for the terrain we – I use 'we' here loosely as I had to do nothing other than be a burden – were having to traverse. The ground was much more uphill and down dale in this part of the woods which, while fabulous fun when exploring it on horseback, was less so when trying to cross it hampered by a large load. For me it was a bumpy ride, something I could hardly complain about, as I had it so much easier than everyone else, plus every step took me closer to her, and that was what I focused on. I couldn't think about the possibility of confronting our enemies. I consciously tried to hope that we wouldn't have to, that they'd magically disappeared and we'd progress straight to the Manor, but I knew I was deluding myself. It was a matter of when, not if, and I had no doubt that until we came across them we wouldn't stop hunting.

It was difficult to judge how long we'd been going but as every minute passed the tension in our group racked up a notch, each minute bringing us closer to our prey. Although this was a hunt with a difference – there was no sneaking up on them, we wanted them to know we were coming.

Five minutes.

We had other cover in place. We'd been surrounded while in the tree house, our protection keeping low, out of sight and spread out. While we travelled the path through the woods, there were others out there at a distance, following and ready. I occasionally caught a glimpse, a shadow and nothing more, between the trees.

But each of these sightings added to my stress, making me jumpy, my breathing shallow. Who was that? Was that them? Straining my eyes I peered into the trees, all this keeping me on high alert as adrenaline coursed through my body.

I had my back to Turner only able to hear his footfall, his breathing. I could see Greene though and never having seen her in this light before it was a surprise. Concentrated, serious, ready for action, she carried her weapon across her body and remained watchful as we moved through the woods.

It was gloomy now, damp and earthy. I could smell, almost taste, the loamy soil. The canopy blocked out much of the light, though I suspected the sun was obscured by clouds and darkness was coming. In the cool evening tendrils of mist reached out along the bottom of the valleys in the uneven ground. I wished we were travelling more quietly, but my companions were making no efforts to disguise our progress through the woods. Announcing our approach we hunted those hunting us – drawing them out.

Ten minutes.

We dropped down a steep incline; I heard twigs snapping underfoot as dislodged soil skittered down the slope with us. I felt Trent stumble slightly then regain his balance as one foot caught in the thick vegetation. Once down the hill, we veered slightly right and followed the bottom of the dip, now thinly veiled with creeping mist, as we aimed to go around the next incline rather than straight up it. But as we rounded the corner, we stopped.

Abruptly.

Orlov stood in the way. Volkov in front of him, held there with a knife to his throat. My stomach dropped – apparently he was not as willing a participant as I'd thought. No pain showed on my father's face; no fear, worryingly, only calm resignation.

A softly muttered curse under Trent's breath was the only outward sign that he was in any way surprised.

He lowered me to the ground gently and I ignored the rush of blood, the light-headed feeling, as he moved to my side and slightly in front. I didn't take my eyes off my father. His features softened, a half smile coming to his lips, which seemed incongruous given his situation.

"Emma," he said. His hoarse voice cut off before he had a chance to say anything further by Orlov roughly pulling him up, the knife digging in, blood beading along the steel. I was shocked to see him this vulnerable.

"Good to see you again, Emma," Orlov inclined his head, "Trent." Three other men were with them, all armed. Ugly was the only other one I recognised from the night of 'the incident', but from Turner's sharp intake of breath to my right, I guessed Anatoly stood alongside Orlov.

"Orlov, Anatoly." Trent's only acknowledgement.

"Drop your weapons," came from Anatoly, his voice deep and rasping, his accent running through the words like hard liquor had roughened the edges. He was shorter than Orlov, broader across the shoulders, and everything about him was dark: his hair, his eyes, his pockmarked and scarred face.

Turner bridled next to me. I felt him tense as if ready to spring and he made to take a step forward, the briefest of movements, and all attention snapped to him. Guns rose as tension as taut as a piano wire sprang between our group and theirs. Trent's arm came up across me, his hand outstretched, his fingers splayed, halting Turner immediately.

"Do as he says," was Trent's command as he withdrew his own handgun and threw it to the side where it landed with a thud in the leaf litter. I could feel Turner's frustration as he and Greene dropped their weapons.

Anatoly grinned as he looked at my neighbour. "Well now, look at you, Turner, all grown up and growling back at me." And he laughed briefly as I felt Turner bristling with fury, no doubt every humiliation he had suffered at the hands of the man coming back to taunt him.

"Steady," growled Trent, his voice low for Turner's benefit, but I could tell Turner was struggling. I remembered the time in the gym, the red mist descending as he attacked me, and now I brought my hand up and placed it on his forearm. It broke his concentration for only a split second, but long enough for him to gather himself again. The once-broken boy grew in stature, his attitude, his control giving me strength.

Orlov smiled his dead-eyed smile, his scar puckering his lip. He muttered something over his shoulder which made Ugly step into position behind Volkov. It appeared his hands were tied behind him, his shoulders pulled uncomfortably back. Orlov removed his knife, sliding it into his belt before pulling out a handgun from the back of his trousers and taking a step in our direction. The men behind him were on high alert, keeping us in their sights, darting glances out into the woods, knowing there were others as they kept cover over Orlov. I wondered if anyone would take the shot while he was open, but calculated no one would. The only result would be us all dying, and quickly.

My thoughts flitted briefly to Baby. I hoped by now she was safely at the Manor and pushed thoughts of her growing up without us out of my mind.

"You know you can't protect her now, Trent," Orlov goaded. "It's over."

His eyes never left mine as he crossed the space between us then raised his gun. As he reached us he pressed it casually against Trent's forehead. It had started raining again, fat drops falling all around. I could hear them pattering off the leaves above. I glanced up at the cold steel which chilled me to the bone more than the pervading damp could ever do.

"You need to get this close in order to be sure of a hit, do you, Orlov?" Trent taunted, which I thought brave, or stupid, given the circumstances.

"Don't worry, Trent, when your time comes I shall be sure not to miss."

"You'll never get another chance as good as this, Orlov. I'd take it while you can." I didn't know why Trent was baiting him like that but I liked his irreverence and I could see it got to Orlov, a flash of annoyance as he bit back.

"Too easy, Trent. I want you to suffer and that means making you and Volkov here watch her die first." Orlov's gaze had still not left me, my insides liquefying at his words, my knees weakening as he stepped closer to me.

Near enough for me to feel his breath on my face. Refusing to show him my fear, not wanting to give him the satisfaction, I glared steely-eyed at him.

"Such a waste," he murmured, his voice so low it was meant for me alone. Though Trent heard, I could tell, his body stiffening in response. Bringing his spare hand up to my face Orlov trailed his fingers across my cheek, along my jawline, brushing his thumb across my bottom lip. I saw his pupils dilate as he inhaled and I curbed my desire to bite it. Keeping the gun up against Trent's head, he moved his hand down my neck onto my chest, my breast. I didn't react, stifling my desire to flinch away from him as my skin crawled beneath his touch. He proceeded to run his hand slowly down my body. I never lost eye contact with him, so saw his reaction as his hand stilled on my empty belly.

"You've had the baby?" This was news to him, which pleased me. It meant they hadn't come across Carlton and Baby in the woods.

"Yes."

"Boy or girl?"

"None of your business."

Anger flared. I saw it in his eyes, but I didn't respond to his reaction.

"Boy…or…girl?" he repeated slowly as if I hadn't understood the question first time around. He adjusted the gun against Trent's head, which disturbed me.

"Girl," I muttered, despising the weakness in my voice.

"Congratulations, you must be very happy." He smirked and I didn't trust his crocodile smile, then leaned in closer, almost conspiratorially as he continued, "And where is your little girl?"

I shook my head. "I don't know." My voice barely more than a whisper.

"You don't know?" Repeated with mock surprise, he then spoke as if we were just fooling around, but I knew he meant business. "Now, Emma, you wouldn't be hiding her from me, would you?"

I didn't reply but stared daggers at him.

He spoke louder now, talking back to Anatoly. "We have another challenge before us, Anatoly, another daughter to find." Then back to me. "And imagine what fun we'll have with her when we find her." From the corner of my eye I saw Trent's jaw clench, the only outward sign of the anger I knew boiled inside.

Though nothing matched the fierce rage that now surged through my body – our baby had been threatened and the protection of our daughter was now all that mattered.

"You will never have the chance to lay a finger on her, we will see to that," I spat out though gritted teeth. His eyebrows rose in surprise at my threat which had been uttered at a time when we were hardly in a position to carry it out. I could see he thought he had the upper hand and I had to agree with him, things did not look good for us. But I had every faith and felt strong, my anger making me so, and we stood together.

"Really, Emma? We'll see." He was so full of himself, so confident, and I wavered, something jagged in my throat. "I wonder if she will be as beautiful as her mother." Orlov spoke softly, bringing his hand up again and stroking the backs of his fingers down my cheek; as he did so his voice filled with such longing he almost had me believing for a moment he was going to relent, but then he chuckled softly and took a step back. Obviously feigning sorrow, he said, "It's a shame, isn't it? Another little girl is going to grow up an orphan."

Though shaking with fury at the threats made against Baby I still felt tears pricking at the backs of my eyes and I swallowed, wanting to wash them away and not let Orlov see my distress. I didn't know what Trent had planned, or how this was going to work out, but the odds did not look good for us. Again I hoped Carlton had got our baby safely up to the Manor and that she was being well looked after. I couldn't allow myself to think about never seeing her again.

My thoughts turned again to the others watching us, surrounding us. Would they attack? Was that the plan? Realistically, probably not with Volkov being held where he was and with us so close. The collateral damage would be too high a price.

Orlov dropped his gun away from Trent's head and started to walk back to the others. His cocky arrogance showed in the way he was willing to turn his back on us, as if we posed no threat to him, and I feared what was going to happen next.

Ugly relinquished his position behind Volkov and I watched as Orlov took his knife back out, only this time he held it against Volkov's back as he wrapped his arm across his upper chest so there was no chance he could make a run for it. Volkov's face strained, and I suspected he could already feel the pressure of the blade.

We were in a standoff. The tension crackled around me, and unarmed I could see no way out. Unable to believe they would kill me in cold blood, my heart was racing, pounding in my chest. My limbs weakening as my heartbeat increased.

Staccato images played, black and white recollections, muddled snapshots of my life; horses, Alex, Eva, Susie, Trent, Carlton, Greene, Sophia, Reuben; Trent rushed through my mind again then more of Eva…as a baby, Eva…growing up, Eva…smiling, turning away from me.

Turning away from me?

Ephemeral and fleeting, Eva's smile haunting as she turned to go…*leaving me*? I'd prayed for death so often since she had been taken, my life no longer of consequence until now, until this moment, until just when it appeared my prayers were about to be answered. This pivotal point when I now had everything to live for and yet, reliant on the plans of others, had no idea how I was to survive this and get back to Baby.

The pressure increased in my head; a roaring silence in my ears distanced me from the inevitable. I didn't know who would blink first, and despite my wish to appear strong I started to tremble. I was to be the first to die, and if that was going to happen, now was the time...

Not giving Orlov or Anatoly a chance to begin talking again, Volkov spoke, his eyes finding mine as his voice distracted me, bringing me back to the dreadful present. "Congratulations." It felt like a ridiculous thing for him to offer given the situation he was in. Then he hesitated, glancing at Trent who stirred beside me. Trent brought his hand back and wrapped it around my arm, squeezing it tightly before letting go, signalling a goodbye as he imperceptibly moved a little further away from me. Exhaling a held breath, he prepared, gathering himself, energy radiating off him as muscles bunched.

"Look after her," Volkov continued, and although he was looking at me, I knew he was talking to Trent and I knew what was coming. Instinctively. I remembered, and understood.

With clarity.

The trap.

The sacrifice.

Tears welled right from my heart, which ached suddenly and painfully.

"No..." I whispered, my voice hoarse and cracking. "No..." louder, and I lunged towards him. Turner threw his arm across me, holding me back, holding me tight. "Please don't, Dad..." and I saw the change as I said *that* word: the tears in his eyes, the smile that shone for me, full of regretful sadness.

"Whatever it takes…"

My father.

The distraction.

He forced himself away from Orlov, bucking against his body, dragging Orlov with him as he crashed into Anatoly, unbalancing him. And I saw the moment on my father's face. I felt it, heard it: the knife slicing through skin, muscle, sinew; steel against bone. A shiver went down my spine and I never took my eyes from him.

Screaming.

And I never took my eyes from him.

I watched the scene unfold even as I felt myself lifted from my feet. Turner had hurled his body into me, in front of me, taking me down with him as a hail of bullets skimmed the air above us.

Trent dropped, throwing himself along the ground, his hands outstretched, grabbing his gun as his body skidded through dirt, soil and debris kicked up in clouds as he twisted and fired simultaneously. Deadly dull thuds rang out.

With precision.

Anatoly…Orlov…headshots. A moment of suspension, disbelief forever etched on their faces, then they fell.

A burst of automatic fire from Greene's retrieved weapon dealt with the other two and it was all over.

The dead and the dying.

I pushed myself away from Turner and scrambled to my feet, crossing to where my father lay. Ignoring Trent's order for me to stay back until the deaths were confirmed, I fell to my knees in front of his body. My hands shook and I didn't know what to do. His face was ashen, the knife still protruding – a gasp as he struggled for air, still alive. I yelled for help, and it came running. All those shadows around us becoming solid shapes and guided by Stanton, they picked Volkov up as if he were something precious then headed to the Manor.

We followed, me in Trent's arms again, Turner and Greene in line. Carlton – Carlton? My brow furrowed as, dazed, I asked where Baby was. Safely at the Manor, he reassured me. That was all I needed right now and I fell silent, watching, following the procession that carried my father out of the woods.

Dusk was falling fast, the light fading to a misty blue as we crossed the parkland. I shivered with the chill in the air and Trent pulled me closer, kissing my head, telling me that everything was going to be all right.

I wasn't so sure.

Stanton instructed those carrying Volkov to take him for assessment in the office. I was taken to a smaller sitting room, Trent finally putting me down once we were inside. Much to our relief, there sat Grace with Baby in her lap, and Mrs F, Bray and Lawson paying close attention. As we entered they looked up, the relief showing on their tense, pale faces. Baby was still asleep, and although I watched her, Grace kept hold of her as Bray and Lawson checked me over. I knew I was bleeding, but brushed their concerns away. That was going to have to wait for the time being. I wanted Volkov to meet his granddaughter, a more pressing need.

Trent carried Baby to the office which had been temporarily taken over by Stanton and his team. I was surprised when I entered to find everything calm. I'd imagined frantic efforts being made to keep my father alive, and for one terrible moment I thought I was too late, that it was already over, but that wasn't the case.

I saw my father lying on his side on a settee and knelt on the floor beside him, checking him out as I did, seeing the knife in his back. I looked up at Stanton, silently indicating towards it, wondering why it was still there.

He replied solemnly, "He will bleed out if we do." I understood. Better facilities would be needed. I gazed at my father's face. His skin was pale with a waxy sheen to it, though peaceful.

"We've brought someone to meet you," I said softly. His eyes opened, his smile looking tired as Trent lowered Baby into my waiting arms before sitting on the coffee table close to me. I tilted her towards my father, pulling back the blanket from around her face so he could see her clearly.

"She's beautiful," he murmured, his words slurring as his eyelids drooped slightly, "like my Zafrelia Rosa."

"What?" I asked, confused, realising thankfully that he was doped up on pain medication. "Who?"

He frowned, then blinked in a moment of clarity. "Sorry, forgot you didn't want to know."

His eyes closed, opening as I questioned, "My name? That's my name – my real name?" I whispered it under my breath – Zafrelia Rosa. It felt too exotic, too unusual. Zafrelia Rosa Volkov was who I'd been born to be, but it didn't feel like me.

"Zafrelia for my mother, Rosa for yours..."

"It's a beautiful name." Although it no longer belonged to me, I wondered and glanced up at Trent, raising my eyebrows at him.

"It will suit her," he agreed, smiling down at me. So much for tradition.

I looked back at my father. "Here's a new Zafrelia Rosa for you to get to know." He smiled, his eyes sleepy.

"That's good. I'm so proud of you, Emma. Spending even this short time with you has been more than I could ever have hoped for. I wish I'd made better decisions earlier..."

His voice tailed off and I glanced anxiously up at Stanton. "How long until the ambulance gets here?"

A deep pause. "There won't be an ambulance," came quietly from Stanton. *What?* I looked up sharply. Stanton's expression was regretful, sympathetic. Nodding his head towards my father, he said, "He doesn't want that."

"Why not? Dad, you need to get to the hospital." The pitch of my voice was rising and Zafrelia stirred in my arms, starting to wake up. "Call one now," I ordered to no one in particular, feeling my throat closing as panic started to take over. I felt Trent's hand on my back, then his arm around me, hugging me to him. I turned to him, desperate.

"Make them, Trent, make them get him to hospital." He shook his head as Stanton spoke, firmly now.

"Emma," and I looked up into his kind eyes, "this is what he has chosen. The internal damage is devastating from such a wound."

"But they could try." My voice was raw from the tears that threatened. "You have to try, you can't just give up," I nearly shouted at my father.

His chest heaved with the effort of responding. "Listen to him."

I stared up at Stanton, wanting answers.

"Orlov knew what he was doing, Emma. He drove the knife straight through the spine, severing the spinal cord. With the other damage, the blood loss, Volkov probably wouldn't even make it to hospital. This is what he has chosen."

I couldn't believe it. To have gone through all this…all this emotion…only for what I thought was a start to be about to end.

The bundle in my arms was becoming more agitated in its movements. When I glanced down I saw Zafrelia was screwing up her little face. Sensing a lung-testing session coming from her soon, I looked up at Trent.

"Can someone take her for a moment?"

Carlton appeared on my other side.

"Here, Em, I'll take her. Come on, Zaffy, let's go and get you cleaned up and dressed properly." Trust him to have already shortened her name.

"Thanks," I murmured, struggling to pay attention to what was going on around me, but vaguely aware of how seriously he was going to take his protective responsibilities.

I saw the room was lined with people now. Our friends, our protectors, were waiting, watching in respectful silence, heads bowed in full knowledge of what was happening.

I turned my attention back to my father and tenderly placed my hand on his cheek, his skin cool and clammy against mine, his lips pale. Vaguely aware of the tremor in my hand I ran my fingers up through the thick locks of his dark hair. Fear clutched at my heart as I sensed the icy tendrils of grief reaching for me once more. Filled with regret for all the time we should have spent together and wishing I'd made him immediately welcome when he'd reappeared in my life, I leaned towards him.

"I love you and I'm so sorry." He stirred, his head shaking almost imperceptibly as his eyes opened, his voice coming in a whisper as he struggled to speak.

"Don't…please, Emma…you have nothing to be sorry for. If I could turn back time I'd have run away with you and never left your side." I swallowed with difficulty and heard the distant distraction of Zafrelia's cry, my breasts aching in response, and I willed time to slow, to stop as I tried to capture those last minutes…those seconds…

"You never did leave my side, Dad…"

He smiled, bittersweet.

"Dad," he repeated, "that means everything…"

His eyes closed; his breath shallowed. He struggled for the next one, then nothing.

Chapter 12

Six weeks later...

It was hot, an early blast of summer sunshine. I was just back from my second ride out of the morning; I'd probably overdone it and would ache later, but by my reckoning the quicker I got my body back in shape, the better. I'd been itching to get back in the saddle after so long away and I'd had the best time that morning. I'd washed Regan and Benjy off earlier before turning them out and it was now the turn of Monty and Zodiac. I finished stripping water out of Monty's coat with a sweat scraper then, untying both of them, I led them out to the field and let them loose in the paddock. Leaning on the fence I stood for a moment, watching them both drop and roll then get up and shake before starting to graze.

Returning to the stables I finished getting them ready for the evening, although Turner had been over to do most of the mucking out earlier. Making beds, filling hay nets and water buckets, I glanced over at the cottage a couple of times, surprised I hadn't been joined already by Trent and Zaffy – the name had stuck. I briefly wondered if they'd taken a trip up to the Manor. Zaffy had had a bad night last night; as I'd suspected, she was a light sleeper and consequently our night had been a long one. My eyes felt scratchy with sleep deprivation, but my joy at getting back to doing what I did best overrode that, at least for the moment.

I finished in the yard and crossed to the cottage, bending to scratch Susie's ears as she came to greet me and thinking I'd fix some lunch for when they returned. As

I walked in, though, I knew immediately they were there. I could sense it, and after checking the sitting room I silently tiptoed upstairs, smiling as I gazed in through our bedroom door. Trent was asleep, spread-eagled across the middle of the bed, topless, skin to skin with Zaffy, who lay face down on his chest wearing nothing but a nappy, her legs curled up frog-like. Trent's hand lay protectively across her, and her cherubic face, which faced me, wore an expression of contented bliss, her hand curled into a fist in Trent's chest hair. I couldn't fault her choice in comfortable places to be: it was my favourite too.

I went back downstairs and quickly put some lunch together, knowing it wouldn't be long before she would wake and want feeding – the discomfort in my breasts was telling me that.

A lot had happened in the last few weeks and life was only now starting to calm down a little. I was struggling to come to terms with my father's death. When it had happened I'd collapsed into Trent, who'd held me tight and comforted me as I'd sobbed uncontrollably, feeling my mood dropping as I succumbed to the depths of grief again. Balancing this with the emotional turmoil of a new baby meant I was all over the place. I knew everyone was worried about me so I tried to cover up the worst of the pits and peaks I swung between. I'd barely known Volkov, but initial sorrow for his loss soon became anger for the life we hadn't had a chance at sharing. All those wasted years fed my irritation. Vivid dreams came in which I could feel the heat of his hug, smell his comforting scent, then I'd wake flooded with disappointment, my pillow wet with tears, as I remembered the way he'd made me feel and missed it.

We'd started by getting through all the necessities: a trip to the hospital for check-ups on Zaffy and me; initial statements to the police, who were all over this incident; eventually being allowed home to get showered, clean clothes on and some food inside us. Our desperate need for sleep became an elusive luxury with having Zaffy now and we ended up sleeping in shifts. We staggered as if sleepwalking through the first few days as we tried to deal with everything.

Cavendish delivered Susie back to me and we'd introduced her to Zaffy. She'd sniffed at the strange-smelling bundle and seemed accepting of this new person in our family, but I made sure Zaffy was kept out of her way and Susie's routine stayed the same.

Trent was taken away by the police along with Greene for further questioning. Carlton and I waited, anxious despite Cavendish's reassurances, and while they were back a few hours later, I thought this was going to take some time to sort out.

There had been a debriefing for what had happened. Trent hadn't wanted me to attend, but I'd insisted and once there I'd wished I wasn't. Volkov had suspected the Polzins had been keeping tabs on him for a while and consequently treated his phone as if it spied on him, leaving it in places where he should be and not taking it to places he shouldn't. It turned out the text Volkov had sent me had been the trigger. What I'd thought of as my father listening to me and trying to forge some sort of contact had actually been the start of the countdown to his death.

When Trent had studied the text he saw the code they had agreed. Emma spelt backwards in the first letters of the first and last words of each sentence. Trent hadn't known about the other texts. If he had he would have seen they weren't from Volkov and would have known that he and his phone had already been picked up. Whether that knowledge would have made any difference to the outcome was the subject of some discussion but it was thought probably not.

Volkov had been hoping to avoid running into the Polzins, thinking that was his only chance to survive, but when he'd left the Manor that night then sent the text he'd had no idea they were already in the country and closing in on him. Their suspicions had been raised because the contract hadn't yet been completed, and the text told them everything they needed to know, as Volkov had intended. They'd put their plans into action, but rather than managing to avoid them they'd picked Volkov up almost immediately at his hotel. He must have known they wouldn't approach the estate without having something to barter with should it all go wrong for them.

I was ashamed that I'd misread Volkov so badly, for not believing he'd put me first when everything he'd done had been to give me the best possible chance at survival. It was true once he'd been picked up he'd helped Anatoly and Orlov gain access to the estate, probably in the mistaken hope that they'd let him live, but he must have known they would never do that. He'd specifically led them to the stable yard, knowing the hidden cameras would pick them up and alert the estate to their presence.

The worst thing had been hearing how he had arranged with Trent that if he became involved and the time should come when a decision had to be made Trent was to do everything possible to save me, at the expense of my father's life if necessary. He had made Trent promise and they had agreed on the words – *whatever it takes*. I suspected Volkov knew all along he would be present at the showdown. He knew what was coming.

The funeral was held at the local crematorium. Though there was a good turnout from the estate, it was difficult to personalise a service for someone I knew so little about.

His ashes now sat in an urn in the cottage and I didn't know what to do with him.

The strangest thing happened the day following the service. I received a call from Forster to say there was a Mr Peabody at the main gate for me from a firm of solicitors in London called Bentley, Bartlett and Rudge. None of the names meant anything to me, but as I wasn't alone, Trent already being at the cottage and about to have lunch, I asked for him to be directed to us. We went out to meet our mysterious visitor together. Zaffy, who had just been fed, was settled and in my arms as we waited.

A few minutes later a sleek dark-grey saloon car drove into the yard and I watched as Mr Peabody got out. My first impression was of a rather fussy walrus, caused no doubt by his bushy moustache extending down to his jawline, the clear definition of which was buried somewhere in jowls that flowed smoothly into the collar of his shirt. He wore an immaculate tweed three-piece suit, the jacket of which he did up across a rather portly stomach, but not before I'd spied a pocket watch adorning the waistcoat beneath. Smoothing the jacket down, he picked a piece of lint from the cuff. I imagined he always dressed with care and had chosen this suit specifically because today he was in the countryside. Tweed was what country people wore.

He stepped towards us briskly on highly polished brogues, formally introduced himself, offered condolences on the loss of my father and congratulations on the birth of our daughter and handed me his business card. I had no idea who he was or why he was here, but we invited him in and offered him lunch which he politely declined, saying he'd already enjoyed all the delights The Red Calf had to offer. He did, however, accept a cup of tea.

Susie had given him the once-over and, having no further interest in him, had gone back to her bed. I looked at him then, settled at our kitchen table, and was at a loss as to how to proceed. As he didn't appear to be about to reveal the reason for his visit, instead making small talk with Trent about which roads he'd used to get to us, I decided to come right out with it.

"I'm sorry, Mr Peabody, but I'm not sure why you're here."

"Oh I do apologise, Mrs Trent, a common fault of mine, I'm afraid, not getting to the point." He was so particular and spoke so very precisely it made me smile. "I'm here to discuss the estate of my client," and there he paused, looking between me and Trent expectantly as if we knew.

"Your client?" I prompted.

"Yes. Zakhar Volkov is…was, I apologise, one of mine."

"One of yours?"

He nodded enthusiastically, looking most pleased with himself. "Yes, one of my most esteemed clients."

I wondered if he had any idea what my father did for a living.

"How did you hear that he had died?"

"Ahh, the arrangement I had with Mr Volkov was that he had to make contact with me at a certain time each week. If he did not I could assume he was dead. I'm sorry." He held his hand up and bowed solemnly for a moment as if only then realising how blunt he'd been, but then bouncing back to his previously perky self, he leaned slightly across the table as he whispered conspiratorially, "And at that point I was to put *things* in motion."

"Things?"

"Yes. Now firstly I must apologise for not making it to the funeral. I'm sorry to have missed it, but the weekly check-in was only the day before and by the time I found out the details, alas, I'd missed it." His hands came up as if in supplication and I waved away his apology as he continued.

"I shall be dealing with the estate, which should be wound up pretty quickly as it is straightforward, there being no property and you the only beneficiary." That was the first time it had occurred to me there might be legal

168

stuff to do following my father's death. It was just as well Mr Peabody was on top of it as I wouldn't have had a clue as to where to start. He smiled benevolently at me as if he were a kindly uncle, or at least what I imagine a kindly uncle would be like, and I suddenly thought of something.

"Have you always dealt with my father's legal matters?"

"Yes, I'm most delighted to say I have."

"Then you must know about the inheritance I received when I was eighteen?"

"Ah yes, a fine piece of work of ours, even if I do say so myself."

"How so?" chimed in Trent.

"Obviously there'd been no planning and the timing was all wrong, but we managed to set up the appropriately dated paperwork for the estate to enable Mr Volkov to put the funds in it that he wanted to make available to you in the future. What with that and the other…things Mr Volkov has requested us to do over the years, he has certainly kept us busy. He will be sorely missed. A most valuable client."

I felt for Mr Peabody, I really did.

"I'm sure," I consoled, before prompting, "What other things did my father ask you to do?"

Mr Peabody looked a little uncomfortable for the first time, shifting nervously on the chair like he'd only just realised that maybe he'd said too much. He glanced anxiously between the two of us. I reassured him he was among friends.

"The changes of identity and the moving of the foster parents mostly…" and he coughed to clear his throat. It all became much clearer: this was presumably where a great deal of my father's support network lay.

I leaned forward a little. "Mr Peabody?" His attention snapped back to me. "Bentley, Bartlett and Rudge is not your everyday, run-of-the-mill solicitors' firm, is it?" He shook his head, placing a finger to his lips as if walls had ears. I sat back, not needing to know more. "Okay, so what else do you have to tell me?"

"Not too much, really. I was just to come here, meet you so you have a contact point should you need anything and let you know the work on the estate is in hand. Oh, and I need to give you this."

He reached into the top pocket of his jacket and withdrew a small key which he slid across the table to me. I looked at it and then at Trent, who shrugged, no wiser than I was, and finally back at Mr Peabody for an explanation. "A safety deposit box," he clarified, as if having one was the most normal thing in the world. Which it wasn't in ours.

Mr Peabody left soon after, having given us details of the whereabouts of the box. As Trent and I sat down, finally, to some lunch, we discussed arrangements to go and retrieve the contents which Mr Peabody had assured me contained absolutely nothing of monetary value, so did not form part of the estate.

I was intrigued.

The following week we made an appointment with the appropriate bank branch about thirty miles away. Having left Zaffy with a delighted Mrs F, we took a trip. I hated leaving her, but in my determination not to be an overly protective mother, a couple of hours away was a start and it was good that it was for something so interesting that would distract me. While fascinated about what my father had left, I was also a little apprehensive, wondering what other thoughts and feelings the contents of this box were going to dig up for me.

The thought of a safety deposit box had been an exotic one and I'd had a couple of imaginative daydreams of being led through increasingly high levels of security to the vault itself, but these imaginings turned out to be fanciful notions. Trent and I found ourselves waiting in a small, windowless and blandly beige room containing nothing more than a table and two chairs, cheap ones at that. We'd been shown into the room by a harassed-looking man who'd introduced himself as a something or other in Customer Liaison, but I'd missed the full title. As soon as we were settled with coffees on the way he scurried off, presumably to the vaults, and appeared a couple of minutes later carrying the box. The way he put it down made it look as though it was quite heavy. I couldn't help wondering if the bank staff knew who or what my father had been, but quite honestly the stressed-looking man couldn't have appeared less interested. I sat staring at the box as he excused himself and eventually we were alone.

I'd already taken the key out of my jeans pocket and had been holding it clenched in my fist. "Here we go," I said under my breath as I reached across the table to pull the box closer. I was surprised. "It *is* heavy! What do you think is in there?"

Trent grinned before saying, "Gold bars?"

I looked at him with mock disbelief, inserting the key and turning it as I replied, "I'm pretty certain Mr Peabody would want to know about that." I stood, opening up the lid, Trent standing with me, keen to see what treasures the box revealed.

We weren't expecting what we did find: my mother, or more precisely my mother's ashes, in an urn. A small engraved plaque on it read Rosa Volkov. Well, that explained the weight.

"Ohh!" A little taken aback, I mouthed at Trent, "I wasn't expecting that."

"No," was all he could manage. I lifted out the urn and put it to one side. The first thing underneath it was an envelope bearing my name and containing one folded piece of paper with only a few words on it, which I read aloud to Trent.

> *"Dear Emma,*
>
> *"If you are reading this then I guess Mr Peabody has broken the news to you of my death and filled you in on my life. I imagine you are surprised, if not shocked, and I only wish I'd had the opportunity to talk to you in person and attempt to explain.*
>
> *"I hope that in here you will find some answers to the many questions you must have and that you are not too angry with me.*
>
> *"Apologies for your mother's ashes. It was difficult for me to get them, and once I had I didn't know what to do with them, but you will.*
>
> *"With all my love X"*

It was signed with a kiss. I wondered if he'd pondered long on how to sign off, trying to weigh up what was the right level to hit between the extremes of Volkov and Dad.

"The note's pretty out of date," Trent said. "I wonder when he last had access to this box."

"I'm not sure," I replied as I put the note to one side. I turned my attention back to the box and, as I was about to find out, my history. Each item I touched was revealing. Another pile of photos, some of me, but more importantly several of my parents, both of them, before me, together and apart, young, carefree and, I could tell, very much in love.

Precious things.

My birth certificate – my real one for who I had once been: Zafrelia Rosa Volkov.

A business card for a hypnotherapist.

Trent's eyes widened when I handed it to him. "We'll have to try to find him," he said. All these years on I wondered if there was anything that could be unlocked, but for now I moved on.

A bundle of letters tied with a blue ribbon. I pulled at the ends of the bow, and the ribbon, crisp and fragile with age, unravelled and lay faded and distorted from having been bent into shape for so long. I flicked through the mismatched envelopes, the only connecting feature being my name, all sealed and each with a date in the corner. Some meant nothing to me at first glance, written in my childhood years, but others did.

My eighteenth birthday.

My wedding day – the first one.

Eva's date of birth, and a couple of envelopes further on her death.

Several letters padded out the time until I recognised the date I'd come to the estate.

Last summer, my wedding day to Trent.

Then one final letter dated at the beginning of March.

A box full of treasures. Letters from my father. Priceless...

I sat heavily in the chair, clutching the bundle in my hand, my knees weak. He *had* cared. I grinned at Trent, satisfied for the moment just with the find. I couldn't open them yet. I'd need to build myself up to hear the words my father had wanted to say to me over the years. That would come all in good time.

We had visitors, many, many visitors. Everyone on the estate popped in for a cuddle – with Zaffy, obviously, not with me – and I was particularly delighted to see Sophia and Reuben among them. Grace brought them over as soon as they came home for a weekend break from school. It was strange – at first they came in shy and quiet, I guess not used to seeing me in the role of mother. Sophia gazed wide-eyed at Zaffy as she lay in her pram and cooed over her when I placed the baby in her arms as she sat on the settee. Reuben was less interested in the baby and more in telling Trent all about the new shooting club he'd joined at school. I watched him as he stared up at Trent, idolising him, and they chatted seriously about how to improve cluster groupings on the targets Reuben had been shooting at.

Cavendish and quite a few of the others – Carlton, Greene, Wade and Hayes among them – disappeared. Trent told me they were 'going for a while' as they wanted to bring the rest of the Polzin organisation to its knees before anyone had a chance to step in and take over at the top. They were splitting into teams, hitting the network from different angles, and I knew who wanted to be with them.

Duty. It can eat at you.

Trent fretted, torn between feeling he ought to be with them and wanting to be with me and Zaffy. Bad guys. They have no respect for the private lives of the good and not having a life that could be put on hold I told him to go. Much better for him to be busy getting his hands dirty than waiting at home with us, where the only likelihood of that happening was in dealing with Zaffy's nappies. That didn't suit him at all, and the energy that gathered in him once the others went would be more constructive if it were directed at the enemy.

Zaffy and I got to know each other, got into a routine of sorts, and I enjoyed having her to myself for a couple of weeks. I say *myself* as if it was only her and me, but in reality we had people visiting us frequently. But it was all

174

good: they brought food and they freed up my arms by wanting baby cuddles. The horses had been turned out for a few weeks as we all recovered and while Zaffy entertained her adoring fans I could get out to do the few jobs that were needed. I was going to have to watch it though or she'd end up one spoilt baby.

The evening was our time. I'd bathe her, the warm soapy water relaxing her as I washed the dark hair that curled more each day. Then, when she was clean, fresh and softly pink, I'd dry her and cosy her up in an all-in-one sleep suit ready for the night. She'd smell particularly delicious at that time and we'd curl up in the rocking chair in her nursery and as I fed her I'd tell her stories of her big sister who I wanted to be a natural part of her life.

Turning away from me.

Though I'd questioned it at the time I'd given this freeze-frame image from that most stressful time a lot of thought. I knew Eva hadn't left me, would never leave me. As Trent had once told me, 'if she were still here I'm sure she would have enjoyed having a little brother or sister, and she would have shared you then. She will always have a place in your heart, Em, so don't think of it as you replacing her, but more of her sharing you with someone else', and now I felt her turning away was that she was content to leave me to another who needed me more and I could live with that.

I loved feeding Zaffy just as I had done Eva. It was an exquisite experience, immensely comforting, and I adored the closeness it brought to us. It was in those moments, when a deep feeling of contentment rolled through me, that I realised however elusive happiness was, it had now come to me as an unexpected gift. Happiness can't be forced. No amount of chasing it, setting it as a target or pursuing it as a goal would ever achieve it; neither would material possessions. It was born of small moments, cherished fragments of time with those we love, and I longed for Trent to return to share this with us.

Trent and all the others were now back, mission accomplished, and for the time being an air of relaxation permeated the estate. There was going to be a gathering at the Manor that evening, a barbecue; a chance to unwind but also a goodbye. Turner was leaving us, returning to his naval unit. I was going to be sorry to see him go, but he'd conquered his demons and was ready to move on.

I'd been concerned for him at first, worried he'd feel he hadn't got the satisfactory conclusion he'd wanted by being the one to kill Anatoly. But Trent was pleased with him. However hard it might have been, he'd followed orders. His selfless act, his control in ignoring the opportunity in front of him and putting my safety first, had told Trent all he needed to know. Turner was ready – more than ready, actually, he was raring to go.

It was a good evening, Zaffy being the star attraction, and it was great to see Sophia and Reuben back for the weekend again. Sophia had eventually settled back at her school and was enjoying life again and it was wonderful to see her back to her previous bubbly self. She couldn't get enough of Zaffy and even Reuben took a few minutes to have a cuddle with her. I'd felt a bit distanced from them recently, but was looking forward to the long summer holidays when we'd have plenty of time to catch up on what they'd been up to and ride out together again.

With our new-found need to grab whatever sleep we could, Trent and I were among the first to leave. Saying goodbye, I hugged Turner fiercely to me, thanking him yet again, though with his usual humility he brushed my thanks aside, promising he'd keep in touch.

The following morning I was up and out as quickly as I could manage after feeding Zaffy as I needed to get the horses ridden early. We had an outing planned. Not so much an outing actually, more something we had to do.

I was mounting Regan when Trent came out, Zaffy strapped to his chest in a baby carrier, the pair of them looking adorable. He carried her car seat in one hand and her bag of essentials in the other and he grinned up at me as I asked where he was off to.

"We're going shopping," he announced.

I frowned. "I'm not sure I should let you out looking as gorgeous as you do with her like that. You are pure woman bait."

He laughed. "It's all right, Carlton's coming with me. He can ride shotgun."

I rolled my eyes. Having Carlton with him would only exacerbate the problem. I could imagine the attention they'd garner, and no doubt love every minute of it.

"Have a good time," I laughed, saying goodbye as I headed out the yard, Susie hot on my heels.

They were back by the time I returned from my second ride. After turning the horses out and finishing off in the yard, I went into the cottage for an early lunch. Trent, Carlton and Zaffy had indeed gathered a lot of attention at the supermarket, but they'd had a good time and got the shopping done, so who was I to complain?

We got ready after lunch and set off for Crowthorpe. Another appointment with the vicar waited. I'd contacted him a couple of weeks before and explained what had happened. He was sympathetic, as you'd expect, and he'd known of my orphan status since the time I'd lived in Crowthorpe, knowing I had no family to support me when Eva died. He was therefore interested in the fact I'd found my father, though I didn't share all the details with him, sticking to the basics of what he needed to know. He'd agreed to have a small service of interment so my parents could be buried together.

I knew Cavendish, Grace, Carlton and Greene were going to join us at the church. What I didn't expect was for us to drive into the car park and find it already nearly full. I was astonished, but Trent parked, stopped the engine, then turned to me.

"They wanted to come," he explained, and everyone was there: everyone from the estate, and in many cases their partners.

We got out and walked up to the church, greeting our friends with smiles and hugs as we walked through the crowd. I carried flowers to leave for Eva and Zoe and Trent held Zaffy in her car chair as the others joined in the procession with us. After greeting the vicar, we gathered around the small hole where a casket was placed containing both sets of ashes. As their souls were laid to rest, I hoped my parents were reunited, wherever they were.

As we drove away from the churchyard I asked Trent to turn down the road where I used to live. I usually avoided it, though had shown it to Trent once before. We slowed as we approached and Trent pulled the car over, coming to a stop on the other side of the road.

Silently we both took in the 'For Sale' sign planted firmly in the front garden of the place I'd once lived with my family – my other family. This was a surprise for him. I checked on Zaffy, who was gurgling in her car seat, before I looked back at Trent who met my eyes, a slow smile coming to his lips.

"It's time?" he said and I nodded, knowing this would be a good moment for him. I was cutting all ties, finally ready for him and our family to be everything.

"Yes." Even now as I looked over at the house I could see us, as we had been: the door opening and Eva bouncing out, excited and raring to grasp whatever the day had in store for her, calling for me to follow. I'd rush to catch up, to grab her hand before she left the garden. I'd turn to see Alex pull the door closed behind him as he joined us on whatever adventure we were embarking on.

I swallowed and blinked away the tears before turning once more to Trent, smiling brightly, knowing my eyes were shiny.

He leaned over to kiss me, his lips soft against mine, then pulling back he used his thumb to wipe an escaped tear from my cheek.

"Susie will be wondering where you are so let's get you home," he murmured, "back to our peaceful and secluded life."

Putting the car in gear, he looked back over at me, shaking his head – amazed no doubt at me managing to surprise him with this. As he gave me one of his broadest smiles, I grinned back, chuckling lightly.

"Ahh, don't start dreaming of a quiet life, Trent," I said as we started to pull away. "That's one we're never going to know."

The End

As promised at the beginning, there now follows a little added extra: another voice, another time.

First, though, a warning, or two.

If bad language offends you, read no further.

If you have been perfectly happy seeing things only from Emma's point of view and have no wish to see what Trent thinks, stop right here.

You have been warned, so proceed accordingly.

That First Weekend

I wait for her, as always.

Her eyes blink open and fix on me. A startling but dazed blue.

I've been hanging around a couple of hours for this moment, ever since the trip in the ambulance. The last hour I've sat right here, the cold remnants of the foul liquid that passes for coffee from the machine on the table at my side. Keen to move from the chair I've moulded into, I get up to go to her.

Welcome back, I say, and I hear the relief in my voice as I ask how she's feeling.

Sore, is her croaky response, which is no surprise.

Regan? she whispers, and I think that's bloody typical of her to ask about him first.

He's fine, back in his stable. I try to reassure, adding that Carlton's in charge because I *know* she'll want to know that.

Her nod causes her to cry out in pain, a reminder of her situation, and she wants to know what the damage is.

You've been lucky, I tell her, though it might not feel like it at the moment. You have a head injury and concussion; your riding hat was smashed. You have extensive bruising across your back and the rest of you is going to be pretty sore for a few days where you hit the ground, but there are no broken bones and no internal injuries, so, like I say, you've been lucky...and I force myself to finish brightly.

But I'm not at all happy this happened in the first place. Bloody horses. Don't get me wrong, I like them, but at a respectful distance, and I wish she had nothing to do with them. And I know that makes no bloody sense at all because that's her job, but I want to protect her. It's as simple as that.

She clears her throat and takes a sip of water from a beaker I pass to her. That's good, she says, speaking more clearly now. I don't know if she's talking about the water or her status update, but it doesn't matter because her voice wraps around my senses, soft in tone with a broken edge like silk snagging across rocks, and it distracts me instantly.

Her frown comes suddenly and she gasps.

My concern is there, in my voice, when I ask what the problem is.

Is she here as well?

Who? I question.

The woman...was she injured by Regan?

She stares at me and I know I'm frowning, confused by her questions. I tell her there was no one else there when we found her.

And now it's her turn to look bewildered as she tells me she was sure there was a woman who had leapt out, which was why Regan had shied...and she tails off, deep in thought.

I ask her what this mystery woman looked like, trying to be helpful, thinking it might jog her memory, though I'm sceptical of there being any memory to jog.

I can't remember, she murmurs. It all seems so vague now. If she wasn't there when you got there, she obviously wasn't hurt, which is the main thing I guess.

If she even existed...

Are you sure your mind isn't playing tricks on you? Could it be a dream you're remembering? I think I've made a good point there.

Mmm...perhaps, she mumbles, her thoughts elsewhere. Maybe it will come back to me.

Then, true to form – true to the Emma I know and...well...know – she turns her attention fully back to me and wants to know if she can go home. Direct, that's Emma. It's one of those traits I like.

The doctor is due to come round and see you again soon, and then we'll see, I tell her. She looks down at her hospital gown, so I say her clothes have been taken back home.

Greene came in and brought some clean things for you to wear, I add. When you're allowed to go, that is.

That was kind of her, she mutters.

That's what friends are for, I think, but then she's thanking me for staying too and saying she's sure I have other things I should be doing, so if I need to go and get on with those, she'll be fine.

Not a chance, Emma, I'm not missing this opportunity. Not in this lifetime.

Cavendish has told me to stay so it's not a problem and I'm here to take you home, if they let you out, I clarify. *Always happy to be of service, that's me.*

That's good of you, she says, and thoughtful of Cavendish.

It wasn't exactly his idea.

It'll save me getting a taxi, she finishes.

I'm not sure you would be up to going home in a taxi anyway, I say. You're going to have to take things easy for a while, you know. But I don't think she does know and I watch her for a moment.

We'll see. I'm sure I'll be fine once I get moving, she says. She brushes off the seriousness of the injuries she's sustained then questions how we found her. Pretty much unconscious as she hit the ground, she didn't have a chance to use her phone.

Regan was seen by Porter who raised the alarm, I tell her. We triangulated the signal on your phone and came to get you. And as her brow furrows I wonder if I've given away more of our capabilities than I should have done.

The door opens and a doctor and nurse enter. Pleased to see her conscious, they carry out some tests.

Emma asks if she can go home when they've finished their poking and prodding.

The doctor says yes, but explains as she's suffered a concussion there has to be someone with her for the next forty-eight hours or so in case of any deterioration in her condition.

Her whole demeanour sags with disappointment and she replies that there isn't anyone who can do that because she lives on her own.

And this is my moment.

My time to step up.

I tell them I'll be staying with her for the next couple of days so that won't be a problem. And I hear in the distance, but wilfully disregard, the faint jangle of alarm this raises in her. I imagine she is wondering where my offer came from. I know she is staring up at me; I can feel

184

the intensity of her gaze and I make sure I don't meet those eyes – that piercing blue honesty that I know will see straight through me in an instant if I make that contact.

It's happened before: the day after she nearly took Carlton into her bed. *That day*, Eva's birthday, her reason for drinking too much. She'd asked me why I did all this for her and I knew she was giving me an opening, a chance to come clean, but I bottled it and told her it was my job. But I didn't believe for one moment she'd bought that. Somehow I'm sure she senses my feelings for her however much I try to hide them. She has a way of seeing right into me as if she can open the pathway to my soul where all is bared – where I have nowhere to hide, yet hide I must. I can't let her see, not all that, not yet…perhaps not ever.

The doctor is happy with this solution and takes me to one side to talk through what to look out for.

Emma thanks me for offering to do this, like it's some great hardship or something. I'm thinking I need to lower her suspicions that there might be an ulterior motive so I tell her I'm just following orders and she visibly relaxes. I bet she's wondering if Cavendish has made me volunteer. *No, Emma, that was all me.*

We move on. Her pain is obvious as she sits up and wants her clothes. Time to inject a little fun I think as I hold up her tracksuit trousers and try not to smile, raising my eyebrows at her as I ask if she wants some help.

True to form, she scowls back at me, no doubt relieved they left her with her pants on. She mutters that she's not sure me helping her dress is entirely appropriate.

You're probably right, Emma, you're probably right.

Then she asks the question I hoped she wouldn't.

Couldn't one of the girls come and help instead? I don't want to lie to her, and this is only a white one, I convince myself, although a considerable amount of effort has gone into making it such.

I look at her and sound genuinely sorry when I tell her that everyone is busy with the Ball coming up. As I'm the least useful person on the estate for the time being, I'm afraid she's stuck with me. I see the moment she gives in, her body – *that* body – relaxing as she begrudgingly agrees she might need some help. But limited help. Let's not go crazy – remember this is Emma we're dealing with here and she doesn't *do* help.

Grumpily she asks me to bring the clothes over to her and says she'll manage from there. I watch her struggle to pull on her trousers when it would be so much easier for me to do it for her. Eventually I'm allowed to help her off the bed, then, when the bottom half is finally covered, she sits down, looking pale and more than a little green. I put on her socks and plimsoll's before tying the laces.

Now to the top half, I say as I reach for the sweatshirt and turn to her, unable to hide my grin. She's resisted all forms of assistance for so long I enjoy every minute of her having to be helped, and she knows it, which does nothing to help her mood.

I can manage, she snaps as I go to put the sweatshirt over her head, but moments later she's stuck with it round her neck, unable to get her arms into it.

Enough, I decide, and I take charge.

Turn around, I say, and when she does I undo the fastenings down the back of the hospital gown, revealing a sliver of skin, pale and soft, that I resist the urge to touch.

As I go to slip the gown off her shoulders, she says, don't look at me.

And I don't.

Until she is ready to show me, I don't.

Protecting her modesty.

And saving myself.

I reassure her I have my eyes tightly closed, and I do. And all is quiet between us.

Eventually, with everything covered up, I say, let's go, keeping it casual, keeping it light. I don't want her to feel anything other than comfortable with me. I collect our stuff together and we head out, making detours to sign forms and pick up pills before finally reaching the car park where I help her up into the passenger seat.

We drive back through the farm entrance and she waves to Porter and Summers as we pass, then we're at the stables. It's late afternoon and I help her out of the truck. Susie hurtles over, throws a growling bark at me (I seriously need to work on my relationship with that dog) and leaps at Emma with undeniable joy. She crouches to give Susie a cuddle then struggles to get back up and I feel a flash of annoyance. I should have been quicker to help her, but when she does get upright again she looks over at the yard. Carlton is standing watching her (*of course he is*) and she raises her hand to him and starts to walk over, her progress slow.

I try not to sound impatient or that I'm treating her like a child when I ask her what she's doing and remind her she's meant to be going in for a rest, but I realise I'm probably kidding no one. Of course she needs to see the horse first. I catch her up and gallantly give her my arm to lean on and progress is quicker.

She has a brief exchange with Carlton and I wish she wouldn't. He's a good bloke, a friend, someone who you want to have your back, but right now, right at this moment, he's a competitor. I know they have a thing between them – a *potential* thing. I've stepped in once, stopped her from ending up in bed with him. It was probably wrong, but right for me (*selfish, I know*) because even now, if I think back to that night when I watched as he reached for her, there's a twist in my guts, a flood of nausea, built purely on the fact he touched her. I pulled rank. It was a shit thing to do, I know, but all's fair in love…

She strokes Regan's nose, then opens the door wide enough to get inside and wraps her arms around his neck before stroking her hand down his nose again. He brings his head up and rests his chin on her shoulder. He knows exactly what he's doing as she kisses and nuzzles the softest part, the silky hollow just above his nostril. Impotently, Carlton and I look on. I don't know about him, but a flash of jealousy sparks in me.

Jealous? Of a fucking horse? Seriously, there's no hope for me.

And I cough, interrupting. Then mutter something about having to get her inside now. She gives Regan one last kiss, checks on each of the other stables, then there's another exchange with Carlton before she's back to leaning on me for the journey across to the cottage.

We let ourselves in and I tell her to go to bed. That's a mistake: I should know by now not to tell her to do anything. And she looks up at me in her weakened condition, ever so slightly like she's pleading with me, wanting to stay up for a bit, watch a film and have some supper. And she's so damned gorgeous, looking at me like that, and I relent. Of course she can do that. That is, after all, exactly what I want: more time with her.

I help her through to the sitting room. I take off her plimsoll's, get her comfortable on the settee with additional cushions and a fleecy blanket to wrap around her feet and legs. Proper boyfriend stuff. Susie comes in at that point and huffs a couple of times, presumably on finding me here, then flops down on the floor as close to Emma as she can get.

I go to sort out something for dinner and find that Mrs F has been a star. What would I do without that woman? Emma is fine with the pasta dish so I stick that in the oven before I return to the patient to see what film she wants to watch. But she gives me the choice. I'm the guest, she says.

I look at the shelf of DVDs and am delighted, but not surprised, to see they are all dark thrillers, violent action and adventure – I didn't have her down as a romcom kind of girl – and I choose the first part of an action trilogy that I've seen before.

She asks if I need to go and get anything from my place before we get settled. Already done, I assure her. It's all in the planning, I think, all the business carried out before she was even conscious. I spread myself out over the other settee and get comfortable. We pause only to eat, and I like the fact she watches the film in silence. There's no need for us to talk, and that feels good. I glance over at her a couple of times and wish I was lying with her. I notice she's falling asleep and only just makes it to the roll of the credits.

At that point I jump up and say I'm off to run her a bath – doctor's orders. When I come down I can see how exhausted she is. I unwrap her from the blanket and, as her muscles have stiffened, help her up.

We get into the bathroom which is when it gets awkward as she wants me to leave. I try to explain that she can't be left alone in the water in case she passes out, but she's having none of it.

She suggests I sit outside with the door open while she gets in and I tell her that works for me, but she'll have to keep talking otherwise I'll be in to check on her. So I take up my position outside the door and sit on the top step of the stairs, my back against the wall. I try not to think about her getting naked (*that body*), but when I hear the movement of the water it becomes more difficult.

Imagining the warm silky water caressing her skin, I look for a distraction and ask her what she wants to talk about. And she suggests we could use this enforced time together to find out a bit more about each other.

Uh-oh.

But I respond with a yes, we could.

I picture her sitting, leaning up against the end of the bath, deep water, soapy bubbles gliding over her limbs, warming her. She interrupts my thoughts to say that, as I have the advantage of having done a background search on her, she'll ask the questions to start with, if that's okay with me. Although I hesitate, of course I want her to know more about me. I want her to know everything – *eventually* – and I'm fucking delighted she wants to.

That's fine with me, Grayson, fire away.

Where do you live? she asks.

I tell her I have an apartment in the Manor and a bit more about the other houses and flats on the estate, realising she probably doesn't know the setup.

Have you always lived there alone?

Yes, I answer, then I wonder, is she probing about the state of my singledom or is that my imagination? *Tell her then, for God's sake, you want her to know.* So I continue, I moved on to the estate after my marriage broke up.

How long have you lived there?

About five years.

That's a long time for you to have been on your own, she comments.

Yes, it is – and you should know. *Aren't you being a bit hypocritical, Emma?*

Well, we're not talking about me, are we?

Indeed we are not, consider me duly reprimanded, I say with a smile. My apologies for interrupting your flow.

Well, she says, you're not that bad looking, and she's teasing me, I know. *Is she flirting?*

You're too kind, I reply, but that's a statement, not a question, and I believe you're laughing at me again, Grayson. I chuckle, letting her know that's fine with me. *Keep it light, Trent. Trent? Since when did you start referring to yourself in the third person, you dickhead!*

I wouldn't dream of it! she replies, sounding all wide-eyed and innocent. Then she carries on, but it begs the question, doesn't it? Why no one else? In that length of time, makes you wonder what's wrong with you.

Does it?

I hadn't considered the possibility before now that there was anything wrong with me, I say. Hoping that doesn't sound too arrogant, I finish with a smile and say, thank you for bringing it to my attention.

I'm nothing if not a gentleman.

You're welcome, she says. And I know she's teasing again, but I'm going to give her something now that she won't be expecting.

And I tell it to her straight.

It's simply that no one has come along who's sparked my interest – at least no one who has been enough of a challenge, which is what attracts me.

Silence.

And I think for a moment that she knows; that I've said too much; that I've blown it already. Just at the point where I decide she must be out cold, and I need to get in there because she's sinking below the water, I hear, what was your wife's name? and we're back on track again.

Zoe.

Do you still see her?

No. *But I like the fact that you're interested, Emma.*

What work do you do with Cavendish off the estate?

Nice try with the change of tack, but I'm not ready to share that just yet.

I'm blasé when I tell her I think she's asked enough questions for one evening and show concern that she doesn't shrivel up like a prune. I go to grab the towel I've left warming for her on the range (*yes, I am that good*) and I warn her against drowning in the meantime.

I take the towel in to her, holding it up to cover my eyes, and leave her to get dry. When I next see her she's wearing pyjamas that she manages not only to look adorable in, but also as sexy as hell – how does she do that? I dose her up with painkillers and leave her to get

192

into bed, but she's pretty much asleep before her head hits the pillow.

I can't sleep. I put the dog out. I lock up. I watch some shit TV. I try to make a fuss of Susie, who's having none of it (she's a tough nut to crack, that one. I can sense she's suspicious of my motives for being here), and I read. I go to bed and read some more, a lot more, but I know sleep is not going to come. *Not with her so close.*

I get up, wander out onto the landing and look in at her door. She's spark out. My sleeping beauty, and I don't use that term lightly. She really is a beauty; not of the pampered, highly polished, plucked, buffed, made up and perfumed variety, but a natural, and what makes her even more attractive to me is that she has absolutely no idea how beautiful she is.

Her hair, which she'd call brown, is so much more than that. It's lustrous and auburn; golden-red streaks in it catch the light, but more often than not it's a mess – like now – stuck up all over the place. I've seen her take her riding hat off when it's hot and put her head under the yard tap before running her fingers through her hair, saying with a brief laugh she's livening it up. *And I want to run my fingers through it too.*

Long thick eyelashes lie across pale skin that so often betrays her feelings. She blushes and it's endearing. Her colour rises with her temper and that is a glorious thing to behold. I remember the first time we met when she went for me over Susie and that challenge turned me on. That was the moment when I knew. Right there, right then, I knew.

And her lips…those lips. Their lush fullness always captures more of my attention than it should. I take a seat in the armchair to watch her for a few minutes, just to check she's all right, and I try not to imagine what it would be like to be in that bed right now with *that body*. Lean, fit and toned. The gym clothes she wears cover everything yet leave little to the imagination, and here and now it's difficult not to think of how it would feel to be skin to skin with her, that body arching into mine; warm, soft, firm. I feel myself stir and force all thoughts of a more salacious nature to the back of my mind because despite the sexual tension she provokes in me I'm at peace here. When I'm with her everything feels right and I'm at ease. I know I could eventually nod off in the chair, comfortable in her presence, but I don't want her to find me here in the morning.

She wakes once, when she turns over, and stares straight at me. I freeze, expecting her to say something, but barely awake she lies her head down and is straight back to sleep.

I glance at the ceiling as I hear a creaking of floorboards. She's up. Flicking the kettle on, I finish getting her breakfast ready. By the time I get upstairs she's back in bed, and despite my sleepless night I aim for positive when I ask her how she's feeling.

She replies that she's sore and grumpy, which is frankly not that surprising. The bruising will be coming out and today is not likely to be a good one for her. She tries, unsuccessfully, to get into a comfortable sitting position, so I put the tray down and go to help prop her up. She's so warm as I arrange the pillows behind her.

Pills first, I say as I hand them to her with the orange juice, then rather unnecessarily I add, I've made you breakfast in bed.

She smiles. How do you know what I like for breakfast? *That voice* – smoky as if she has a twenty-a-day habit. It does something to me every time.

Let's see how I've done, shall we? I say, and I grin as I put the tray on her lap then stand back to await her verdict. She looks down: a mug of tea, builder's strength with very little milk.

No sugar? she enquires.

No sugar, I confirm.

Two pieces of toast with marmalade – perfect. Well done. Good guesswork.

Good detective work, you mean, I say, though it wasn't difficult. Her kitchen is hardly packed to the rafters with every type of culinary ingredient known to man. There's only what she uses and no more. Bread, marmalade, teabags, milk – semi-skimmed.

Can I sit down? I ask.

Of course, she mumbles through her first bite of toast. I come round to the other side of the bed and sit on it, as casual as you like, so I'm facing her. She's not expecting that at all, I can tell immediately. She's acutely conscious of me being on her bed. I know I make her uncomfortable, that I affect her physically, and we've been circling each other for months – ever since that night in the gym.

She'd landed a blow that doubled me over, then I'd felt her hand on my side, like a brand on my skin, the electricity of that connection jolting us into the reality of what was between us. I was already there, but it was in that moment, like a switch being flicked on, that I saw it in her eyes. I was alarmed at the time; I knew she was a flight risk and I desperately didn't want her to run, so I cooled things down immediately, happy to wait until she was ready.

However, here and now I'm determined to play any advantage I can, so I look as comfortable and relaxed as possible, and as if sitting on her bed in my pyjamas is not at all strange.

How did you sleep? I ask.

Okay, although I woke once to find you watching me. What was that about?

I'm prepared for this and I grin cheekily at her as I reply, well, the snoring stopped so I thought I'd better come in and check you were still alive.

She looks at me in horror before she says indignantly, I do not snore!

I laugh at her horrified expression before responding, good to see you focus on the important part of what I just said.

She finishes her piece of toast, but offers me the second one which I take and dispatch happily as she sits drinking her tea and watching me eat. *Loss of appetite, is that a good thing?*

What plans do you have for the day? she asks.

None, other than to look after you, I reply.

I'm going to get in the shower as I need to wash my hair. I presume you don't need to watch me do that as the likelihood of me drowning is minimal.

Funny girl.

Your sarcasm is not lost on me, Grayson. That'll be fine, but don't lock the door, will you, just in case? You're likely to be stiffer than yesterday, so if you need help in dressing you'll have to call me. I'm going to leap in your shower first, though, if that's okay?

And I go to get my towel from my room and spend a few minutes 'enjoying' a cold shower, if that's possible. I think it's probably best if I stick to those while I'm here. She's having an unfortunate effect on me and I'm up and down as often as the Oblivion ride at Alton Towers. I could do with a run, burn off some of my excess energy.

I dry myself then walk out with the towel slung round my hips, but the show's wasted as she's turned away from me, getting off the bed. *Shame*. It's been obvious to me over the years that women find me attractive. Any women; all women. I've never had any difficulty in getting them horizontal, but as I get older I find their eagerness tiresome. Then up pops Emma, the very antithesis of eager, and there has been no one, no one at all, anywhere near me since I met her in the stable yard. She challenged me, and that was that. Pathetic, I know. You don't need to tell me. I'm thirty-five, in my prime, with a tough no-nonsense military trained persona, yet she has me feeling like some overgrown schoolkid working up to a first date. And while I've sometimes wondered if she's guessed at my feelings for her, I don't believe she has the first idea of the extent of the effect she has on me.

I leave her to shower while I dress and clear up downstairs, then I go back up to check she's getting on okay. I should have called out, but I don't as I'm distracted by her groan of pain, and as she doesn't hear my approach she starts when I say, that looks painful, and she glares at me as she covers her chest, snapping and wanting to know why I'm looking at her. I ignore this awkward moment though I'm annoyed I've made her uncomfortable. Don't worry, I try to reassure, your modesty is intact, and I move towards her, offering to help her dress, and she questions softly, what looks painful?

I'm standing behind her as I answer. I'll show you, I say, and in order to do this properly I take a chance. Excuse me a moment, I add and gently ease her tracksuit bottoms down a little so the band of them sits just below her hips. I feel her breath catch.

There's a particularly blackish band as wide as this, I say, and I open up the gap between my thumb and first finger to about four or five inches to show her, bringing my hand round in front of her so she can see. Stretching from here, I tell her, and I put my fingers gently on her shoulder then run them down into the arch of her back and over her natural curve to the opposite hip, to here, I finish, letting my fingers rest on her hip for a moment.

And I still, silently relishing the feel of her skin. Clearing my throat, I carry on, my voice quiet, the bruising extends out from that line through various changes of colour from purple to a yellowy-green. Then there's another bruise extending up from your other hip from where you hit the ground. As I say this my fingers trail slowly across her lower back to the other hip, where again I pause and my breathing deepens.

Christ, this feels so good. My fingers are warm against her skin, which is soft and cool, and she smells incredible: the light scent of body wash, but under that, all her.

And, finding it difficult to swallow, I hold my breath and close my eyes.

It is all I can do not to lean down and kiss her neck. I try to block out thoughts of how that would feel, and fail, wanting to run my tongue along her skin, kissing, tasting, exploring every part of her, completely absorbed in her, in every cell of her being. I feel her shiver through my fingers.

Are you okay? I murmur, my voice thick. I move away slightly. It wouldn't do for her to feel just how badly she's affecting me.

Yes, sorry, just ticklish, she explains, and I can sense how flustered she is as she turns towards me. I gaze at her for a long moment before breaking the spell.

Let's finish getting you dressed then. Promise to close my eyes, I joke, easing the tension between us. I help her quickly, then excuse myself and disappear downstairs and outside. Fresh air is very much what I need, as well as a few moments to regain control of myself. I see Carlton over at the yard getting the horses ready and raise a hand in greeting to him. He replies similarly, but he is busy and doesn't look in the mood to talk, which suits me. I leave him to it and, picking up the papers that Hayes has dropped off for us, I go through to the sitting room and make myself comfortable.

Emma joins me a short while later having told Susie to eat the breakfast I made for her, and that she won't touch because *I* made it for her.

She takes a section of the papers and curls up on the other settee to read. We enjoy some banter; it's been a long time since I've done this and it feels good, natural. We're getting on well, and I suddenly have the horrible feeling that unless something happens soon there is every chance we shall end up falling into the dreaded friendzone. There is no escape from that. And I can't have that. Not at all.

We have only just finished lunch when a message comes in on my phone. I take it out of my pocket to read – *what the hell?* It's an unexpected contact from the past which makes my stomach clench and I look across at Emma. I have to deal with this, and I know I'm distracted when I tell her to go and rest, I need to go outside to make a call.

The yard is empty now and I call Dr Philpott as requested. I pace up and down near my truck, waiting for him to answer but knowing this cannot be good news. This will never be good news. I listen as he tells me that Zoe has absconded from under his care. It's not as if she's in a locked-up facility – *any more* – but she has appointments to keep, which she hasn't, and her prescription hasn't been filled. I ask a lot of questions, most of which he can't answer. While I'm angry I manage not to take it out on him, though I suspect he's fully aware of my mood. He has done me a favour, though: he didn't have to tell me. In fact, he shouldn't have told me, what with all those instructions Zoe insisted on putting on her file. But Dr Philpott is concerned she may come looking for me, and I guess there's a chance of that, but I think it's a slim one.

And then suddenly I realise – and I close my eyes. A cold shiver passes through me and the knot in my stomach tightens. A woman – Emma asking me where the woman was. And I know.

Shit.

I make a call to Cavendish and fill him in. He says he'll come round later, keep it casual, ask a few questions and see if he can get any description. I'm pleased he'll do this as I don't want to. I've already been dismissive of what happened when Emma wasn't able to remember much, and if I open up the conversation now it will raise her suspicions. I don't want to go into my past with Zoe just yet. All in good time on that score, I think.

I go back in, clear up and go through to watch a film, but I see and hear nothing of it. My feel-good feeling has all but gone, my thoughts are deep in the past and now filled with worries for the future. By the end of the film I've convinced myself I've overreacted by calling Cavendish. It couldn't have been Zoe who leapt out on Emma. Why would she have done so? It's not as if Emma and I are in a relationship, mores the pity, and if Zoe was going to go for anyone it would be me. It has always been me in the past, and it makes no sense for her to have attacked Emma.

When the film ends Emma walks slowly over to the yard to check in with Carlton. I watch her from the kitchen window as I call Cavendish again. I tell him I've overreacted, but he disagrees and says he'll come anyway, just to make sure, to cover our bases. He arrives about half an hour later, and brings dinner with him.

Now, not much gets past Emma and I get the distinct impression that she's aware something is up, but Cavendish quickly turns his full enthusiastic attention on and can't apologise enough for what his horse has done to her. She reassures him that it was nothing to do with Regan and goes on to explain to him what happened. He questions her at some length about the woman, but Emma can't tell him much. We're no further forward on that front as Emma seems to doubt her own recollection now, though she's pleased that Cavendish takes her account more seriously than I did. And I hope she doesn't join the dots between the sudden interest and my earlier call.

Cavendish leaves soon after, insisting Emma is not to go back to work until at least the following week, and we say our goodbyes. Then we're alone again.

I get dinner ready – another masterpiece from Mrs F that only requires reheating – and I call through to see if Emma is up to eating at the table, which she is. I make an extra effort and light a candle. She comes through and smiles, tells me how nice it looks. We sit to eat and I offer a bottle. I know she prefers red, and I say, I know you can't drink at the moment, but I asked them to put in this bottle of non-alcoholic wine I thought you might like. Do you want to try some? We can pretend it's the real thing.

Yes please, she says, before offering me a 'real' alternative if I want to help myself. There's no reason you shouldn't have a drink, she adds.

There's every reason, I think, such as not saying too much, or doing anything I'll regret later. But I smile as I reply, I thought I'd join you, show support for the invalid.

She starts with the questions again, wanting to know if I have any family around.

I don't have any family left, I reply. A late surprise for my parents, I was an only child, and they both died a few years ago, so now it's just me.

That's a shame, she says, and she's genuine. Of course she would be, but this doesn't stop me from being clumsy moments later.

Yes it is, I respond, but I had my parents' love and support until I was more than grown up. Losing your parents at the age you lost yours is what's hard…Sorry, that was a bit tactless.

See what I mean? Two feet right in there.

Its fine, it's not something I think about that often, she says, and she honestly does seem okay with it. I watch her for a moment as she eats. The candlelight wavers, contrasting planes and shadows on her face that turn and move as she does. I want to know more.

As it's my turn to ask the questions this evening, I say, I'll carry on with this line, if you don't mind?

I don't mind, ask whatever you like. I'll soon tell you if you've gone too far, she responds, and I know she means it.

Okay then...do you know how your parents died? Nothing like getting right to the heart of a subject, I think.

They died in a car accident, she says, then, occasionally prompted by me, she goes on to tell me about her life in foster care. Women want you to be interested in them, don't they? And I find I am, but it's getting heavy and I'm relieved when she tells me she was moved on so often between foster homes because she was a difficult child, because it gives me an opportunity to lighten the mood.

Ahh, now we're getting it! I joke. You, difficult? I find that hard to believe.

Very funny, she says in that way which means it's not, but she smiles and seems to be enjoying the fact that I'm entertained by this early description of her familiar behaviour. I guess you'll be pleased to know that you're not the only person in my life that I've been difficult with, she continues, as it turns out you're nothing special.

Ouch, that's a bit harsh, and I can see she thinks this too.

Thanks for the reminder, I reply, and I keep my eyes on hers, not letting her off for an instant before continuing with my questions.

What did you do after the foster care ended?

Before I had to leave care I was already with Alex (*Tosser! Still, his loss...*) so we got married at eighteen and I went straight from one to the other. We were able to buy a house because I'd been left an inheritance from my parents' estate.

That was very young to get married, I state.

Yes, and as it turns out quite foolish, she replies, and she sounds sad about it too. Then she smiles and turns the question right back on to me. When did you and Zoe marry?

Early twenties, quite foolish too, I reply. This is another point on which we have trodden on similar ground and I hesitate for a moment, looking away as I gather my thoughts and wonder if I dare say what I want to say – and I find I do.

He hurt you badly, didn't he?

Yes, he did, she mutters, before adding in a falsely bright tone, but now you have gone too far. I suggest we agree not to talk about our failed marriages or before long we'll be wallowing in our mutual misery.

Okay, I agree. Filling our glasses up, I move on to safer territory, winding her up about her rather singular film tastes. She then confesses to having a drawer full of other films – old black and whites, love stories and romcoms – and gives me the chance to choose something from this collection should I wish, but I suggest we finish the trilogy we started.

I clear away dinner and I know she is watching me as I wash and she dries. I take this as a good sign that she wants to be near me as much as I enjoy being with her.

We watch the film, I run her a bath and we go through the same routine as the previous evening. But something has changed. I can feel it: the charge between us is crackling, but I make nothing of it. Keep calm, keep cool, I decide.

I sleep no better than I did the night before, but this time I don't dare go into her room. I stand for a while, leaning against her doorway, and she is restless. I watch as she tosses and turns in an effort to find some comfort, but I don't know if her discomfort comes from her injuries or her thoughts.

I have stuff on my mind and I wonder if I should come clean with her and tell her about Zoe – everything about Zoe and my chequered history in the RAF. I worry that she finds me too serious, but I can't be the life and soul of the party anymore. Maybe once I was like Carlton, but the grief I've suffered over the loss of Zoe, my marriage and my career has taken its toll. We're not so very different, I think. I don't feel good not telling her, particularly about Zoe, but it's not like we're together, is it? Would she expect me to tell her before we have even become anything? I didn't think so, and besides it might put her off. This is proving to be challenging enough already. I make the conscious decision to keep all the bad stuff to myself and agree to tell her if – no, when (*think positively*) we get together.

And if I feel the flames licking at my soul at this moment I choose to ignore them.

I return to my own bed and eventually drift off sometime on the approach of dawn.

You look tired this morning, I comment as I deliver breakfast then sit on the bed again.

I didn't sleep well, she replies.

Perhaps you can have a nap later on to catch up, I suggest.

Yeah, maybe, she says as she makes a start on breakfast, but she looks like she's struggling from the first mouthful. I allow myself the luxury of imagining her lack of appetite is down to me, my presence, but I don't know if that's the reason or how to press my case any further without being bloody obvious.

Sorry, I don't know what's happened to me, she says feebly as she hands me the other piece of toast, which I devour. *No problem with any of my appetites.*

She shoos me out of the room so she can shower and dress, and I wish I knew what's going on in her mind because today I leave and I'm never going to get the chance to be this close and have this influence over her again.

I'm watching the news when she comes down and then I go off for my own shower. When I finish I see she's over in the yard talking to Carlton, which doesn't help my mood. It annoys me that he's the most capable one around here to take over with the horses and I wish I could get someone else in instead. I have to go back to work today and I don't want to leave him here with Emma. I know I'm being possessive, and I know that's not a good trait, but I want her so badly I cannot face the thought of her being with anyone else.

But I have someone else to win over first and I find her in the sitting room, stretched out on the carpet. I get down on the floor and we're head to head. Suspicious of my intentions, she rolls from her side onto her front, her head on her paws, and studies me intensely. Nose to nose we stare at each other and I know I will never win that battle. I hear the back door and the sounds of Emma moving about in the kitchen, boiling the kettle. I hope for coffee. Susie hasn't taken her eyes off mine, in a battle of wills neither wants to lose. Emma comes into the sitting room and stops as she catches sight of us.

What're you doing? she asks.

I'm trying to make friends with your dog, I reply. I have the feeling she doesn't trust me because we got off to a bad start, and I'm still not taking my eyes off Susie. I start to blow gently at her, trying to get her to play, but she's having none of it – she growls once in warning, gets up and walks off, giving a couple of huffs as she makes her way out of the sitting room, making it clear she thinks I'm an idiot.

That's a work in progress, I mutter for Emma's benefit, letting her know I've not given up yet. Susie could be the key to the future of our relationship, I think. If I can break Susie, then who knows? I roll onto my back and stretch before I get up and join Emma for coffee.

Will you be okay if I pop out for a bit? I've got an errand to run, I ask a little later, having got her comfortable on the settee where she is reading a book.

Of course, she replies.

I grab my keys from the table and leave.

I'm back within the hour, mission accomplished, and for some reason as I enter the cottage I'm humming. I'm not sure of the inspiration behind the level of contentment that makes me do this, but it might be because of the potential source of conflict I hold in my hand, showing that, pathetically, I'm willing to grab any opportunity for interaction.

I ask if she wants any tea, and when she doesn't I wander in. Carrying my large paper bag casually, I stop right in front of her. She closes her book and puts it to one side. I don't think she will be able to resist asking, and she doesn't let me down.

What's that?

This is the errand I mentioned – it's a little present for you. There's something in the tone of my voice that makes her eye me suspiciously, her eyes narrowing. I sit down on the other end of the settee and hand her the bag.

Open it, I say, and I raise both eyebrows at her, grinning.

She sits up a little, reaches into the bag and lifts out a large box. I sit back, observing her keenly. I'm eager to see her reaction. She lifts the lid and finds inside a bulky red and black object that resembles something you see the police wearing during a riot. I get the distinct impression she knows exactly what it is, but she plays the game. *Good girl.*

What is it? she asks sweetly, inclining her head to one side and looking straight at me. I am delighted to be given the opportunity to launch into an explanation.

Grayson, I'm glad you ask. This is the Point Two Pro Air Jacket…and she gets the full sales spiel. Once I've stopped spouting, I look at her expectantly, trying to gauge what her reaction will be, though deep down I think I already know.

I see, she says. And you're expecting me to wear this? Her voice rises, and for all its breathy undertones I can sense a very definite edge to it. I could back away now, but I don't.

Absolutely. In fact I insist on it, I say, then add, as if to challenge her, you could almost say it's an order.

I don't have to accept orders, I'm not in the forces, she snaps.

No, they would never have you. You're far too defiant, I retort, and I see the colour rise in her cheeks as she takes a deep breath. *And she looks magnificent.*

Whether you insist on this or not, I don't want to wear it. I've never liked these body protectors, I find them too constricting. And I would not have fallen off in the first place if it hadn't been for that wretched woman coming at me out of the undergrowth.

Though I flinch at that, I reply that we've found no evidence that is what happened. But her saying it has taken the wind out of my sails and suddenly I'm weary.

Grayson, I'm tired of having this argument, I say. I feel protective of you. That's just the way I am and I'm doing what I need to do.

She must be able to see that it is my job; it is important to me to keep her safe.

She's quiet, and for a moment, just a brief moment, I think she's going to relent, though deep down I know she won't. But I get more than I expect – I get an offer.

How would you feel about a compromise? A rich patina coats her voice with its glossy lacquer and I can already feel myself giving in to whatever it is she is about to ask of me. All she has to do is keep talking. I mentally shake myself free of that influence.

You want to negotiate? I think about this. *Playing the game.* Hmm…what are you offering? It is now my turn to look suspicious.

How about I agree to wear this whenever I ride out of the yard? So I needn't wear it when I'm schooling in the arena or the paddocks.

Okay, I think we can work with that, I say, although if you're jumping anything over three feet in height in the arena or paddocks I want you to wear it.

I keep my gaze on her steady, then smile as she exhales with frustration. Clearly she realises I'm not going to give up and she is going to lose this round.

Okay, she agrees, and she sighs wearily but seems reconciled to her fate. I smile briefly and with relief until she continues, and it's red because…? and she leaves the question hanging.

I respond, explaining I reined back on getting the hi-vis one as I didn't think I'd get her to go for that – probably a step too far – so I got the next most violent colour available to make her stand out.

Well, of course you did, she replies with resignation.

At this I give her my broadest smile which she can't help but respond to. Then I announce that I'm going to go and pack my things and I feel my heart sink. If I'm not mistaken it feels like it brings down the whole mood.

Before I leave the room she says, thank you, Trent, for staying here with me. It was kind of you to give up your time. And she is polite, her words strangely formal and not what I am wanting at all.

I know being helped is something you abhor, but I've enjoyed looking after you, I reply. *And we're so frustratingly proper, so fucking British about it all.* Then I hesitate for a moment and gaze at her. I'm standing there, wondering if this is when I should declare myself. Surely I've made my intentions clear, so maybe the signals I think I'm reading are not there at all and all I'll make is a fool of myself and I think better of it because I leave to go and pack.

I don't know what to do. I don't want this, that I do know; I don't want to leave and be no further forward with her. Maybe I haven't made my feelings for her obvious enough, even though *I* feel I've been wearing a flashing banner across my chest declaring all. Maybe it wasn't enough; maybe I should have made a move on her. But I thought that would scare her off. I wanted to be respectful; I wanted to let her come to me, but on her terms when she was ready, and now that is looking like it was a mistake.

Anyway, what if I am wrong and she doesn't feel like that about me? I don't want to be left looking like a complete idiot. However, I know I can't leave it like this. I want to say something; I want to tell her how I feel, and while I'm afraid of looking like a fool, afraid she will reject me, just the thought of that making me feel sick, I know I can't let this go.

As I go downstairs to leave she gets up and meets me in the kitchen.

I hope you have a good trip, she says as she starts to busy herself, looking in the fridge to see what to have for lunch. *Lunch? For God's sake, you're driving me crazy, Emma. We have matters of life and love to deal with here and you're looking for what to slap between two slices of granary.*

211

I mutter something about hoping she continues to improve as the week progresses. Then I glance out of the window towards the empty yard, but I imagine Carlton there, waiting, and add with a grimace, no doubt once I'm gone you'll have the oh-so-attentive Carlton hovering around you, attending to your every whim, and with that I turn to the door.

What is it, Trent? she says. You don't want me, but you don't want anyone else to want me either?

At last...

I stop dead, take a deep breath and turn back to the woman I worship – to the one who has brought me to my knees.

And I say, who said I didn't want you, Emma? Just so there's no misunderstanding, I want you very much, but not until you're ready for me.

I don't take my eyes off her as I wait. *I've bared all of myself to you, Emma, now it's your turn. So come to me; give yourself up to me.*

I feel my stomach clench. I can see her internal struggle, but whatever's going on it's clearly not enough to break her, and I close my eyes and shake my head as despair closes in. I start to turn once more to the door.

Then as if from nowhere, I hear, I am ready for you...

I can hardly believe it. I stop, my heart is beating so hard I can feel it physically pounding in my chest. I look back at her, relief and elation flooding through me, warming as I smile at her, seeing her anxiety dispel as I do so. Before she catches her breath I turn, cross the kitchen and wrap her up in my arms, closing my eyes as I relish the feeling of holding her so close.

Oh God, I can't tell you how long I've been waiting for some indication, any indication, that you feel about me even a fraction of what I feel for you, I murmur in her ear, loosening my arms slightly so I can bring my face up to look at hers. I can see what I hope are happy tears gathering as she looks at me, and as they overflow I bring my hands up to each side of her face and wipe them away with my thumbs. Dropping one hand back to her waist I hold her close as I continue to run my other thumb down her cheek, then gently across her lips, those lips that promise eternity – so full, so ready for me; they distract me and I struggle to swallow. I know if I kiss them I will be going nowhere. For they are the gateway, the threshold over which I must not tread. Not today, not yet…

Do you think this is wise, she says softly, getting involved with someone as messed up as me?

I kiss her cheek, my lips lingering on her skin as I inhale her scent.

I have no choice, I reply. I don't have the strength to keep away from you any longer even if I wanted to, and anyway there are things about me which are just as screwed up. You just don't know about them yet.

I hesitate then, feel myself frown before I continue. Actually, I hadn't thought about that before now, but you're probably taking the bigger risk here, which might not be good for you. You should think about that and decide if this is the wisest thing for you to do.

I have no choice. I don't have the strength to keep away from you any longer, even if I wanted to, she echoes back at me, and she smiles a smile that lights me up inside. I kiss her cheek again, then release her, and sigh as I do so.

I can't believe I have to tell you this now, but I do have to go, I say in a voice filled with regret, and she nods and smiles back.

I know, go on, she says, and I leave, promising to be back as soon as I can. I don't want to go, I really don't, and my mind's buzzing. I curse the fact we've spent so much time here alone and yet not been together, wasted time, but I won't dwell on that now. We have the rest of our lives and I focus on that thought, but everything I still need to tell her comes to the fore, and again I push it to the back of my mind and ignore the flash of anxiety it brings.

I feel her eyes on me as I walk down the path, and while I hate every step I take away from her I am so filled with elation I'm no longer walking, I'm flying, and feeling fucking invincible. I want to punch the air and yell our news to the world, because when I drive off I catch her smile as she returns my wave and I know this is only the start, the very start, of something that's going to be glorious.

Acknowledgements

It is difficult to believe that I'm finally here, at the end of this trilogy, and I have so many people to thank for helping me get this far. So, as they say, somewhere or other, in no particular order...

A huge thank you to all the team at SilverWood Books for copy-editing, proofreading and for designing fabulous covers for me. With an extra special thank you to Helen Hart for being constantly warm and friendly and her unfailing support and enthusiasm from the very first time I made contact with her.

To my Super Six beta readers – Debra Cartledge, Katherine Matthews, Claire Millington, Andrew Moore, Sarah Postins and Kathy Sapsed, many, many thanks. These poor souls have the challenging task of reading the first draft and then telling me the truth. The fact that they do so honestly, albeit at times quite brutally, whilst managing at the same time not to break me is a gift for which I am very thankful.

There have been several of you out there who have helped with various bits on this final book as I've bounced ideas at you but there has been one who has gone above and beyond the call of friendship with their support and helped with taglines, worked on the blurb and provided invaluable feedback on the other voice, so to the Front of my Pantomime Horse and founding member of the Carlton Fan Club you know who you are, and I thank you, although those two little words are nowhere near enough.

To everyone in the online booky-people community that I inhabit, your generosity of spirit in supporting other authors, writers, readers, book bloggers, editors, publishers and all involved in the writing world is astounding. There are far too many of you to name but here's a clue – if you're reading this I'm talking about you and thank you.

To my younger bro, Dave, who via his company, Deeho, has helped with all my website/blog related issues, I'm sorry I never got round to fitting in the alien vampires for you…I appreciated the input – no, really, I did – maybe next time…

To my family, friends and the wonderful community in which I live, thank you. I have barely gone anywhere this year without someone asking me when the next book would be coming out. Even though I haven't necessarily given you the answer you've wanted, your interest has been incredibly encouraging.

To Russell, my better half, for coming up with the fabulous Three Shires Publishing, and for his patience and support as I've wandered off into this bewildering writing world that I long to inhabit forever. Thank you, I would be lost without you.

Contact Details

Thank you for reading this far. I'm always interested to hear from readers with any feedback, thoughts or observations they are willing to make. If you'd like to get in touch, or you'd like to hear about what's coming next you can do so through my website at Georgia Rose Books where you will also have the opportunity to follow my blog. Alternatively you can email me at info@georgiarosebooks.com for a chat or to request to go on my mailing list; follow me on Twitter @GeorgiaRoseBook; find me on Facebook or 'like' The Grayson Trilogy on Facebook. I look forward to hearing from you.

Finally, if you have enjoyed reading this, please tell ~~someone~~ *everyone* you know about it and, whatever you think of it, if you are able to, would you please consider leaving a review? Of whatever rating! You might not think your opinion matters, but I can assure you it does. It helps the book gain visibility and it informs other readers whether or not to purchase it, so if you could take a minute or two to leave a few words on Amazon and/or Goodreads that would be hugely appreciated.

Now, if you're sitting there holding a beautiful paperback in your hand and you're thinking that request doesn't include you...well please think again. It doesn't matter how or where you bought your paperback Amazon and Goodreads will still accept a review from you.

Thank you.

Printed by Amazon Italia Logistica S.r.l.
Torrazza Piemonte (TO), Italy

11407035R00130